THE MYSTERY OF THE
MEXICAN GRAVEYARD

John Bibee

InterVarsity Press

Downers Grove

© 1995 by John Bibee

InterVarsity Press® is the book-publishing division of InterVarsity Christian Fellowship®, a student movement active on campus at hundreds of universities, colleges and schools of nursing in the United States of America, and a member movement of the International Fellowship of Evangelical Students. For information about local and regional activities, write Public Relations Dept., InterVarsity Christian Fellowship, 6400 Schroeder Rd., P.O. Box 7895, Madison, WI 53707-7895.

Cover illustration: David Darrow

ISBN 0-8308-1913-4

Printed in the United States of America ∞

Library of Congress Cataloging-in-Publication Data

Bibee, John.
    The mystery of the Mexican graveyard/John Bibee.
        p.   cm.—(The Home School Detectives)
    Summary: When Carlos and Julie Brown go to Mexico with their
parents to help out at a village orphanage, Carlos investigates the
ghost sightings, strange illness, thefts, and other mysterious
events that threaten to close down the orphanage.
        ISBN 0-8308-1913-4 (pbk.)
        [1. Mystery and detective stories.   2. Drug traffic—Fiction.
3. Orphans—Fiction.   4. Christian life–Ficton.]   I. Title.
II. Series: Bibee, John.   Home School Detectives.
PZ7.B471464Myf   1995
[Fic]—dc20   95-33595
                                                                              CIP
                                                                              AC

16	15	14	13	12	11	10	9	8	7	6	5	4	3	2	1
08	07	06	05	04	03	02	01	00	99	98	97	96	95		

Chapter One

The Ghost in the Graveyard

Carlos and Julie Brown and their friends were walking up a narrow cobblestone street in the little Mexican town of Santiago when they heard the scream. They were near the top of the hill by an old abandoned church. The church stood on the land next door to the orphanage. They paused, listening. All they heard was the wind, which had picked up rapidly since they left the birthday party fifteen minutes earlier.

The party for one of the children in the orphanage had been in the town plaza. The customs at a Mexican birthday were different from the birthday parties back in Springdale, but Carlos and his sister had just as much fun. Carlos himself had delivered the final blow to the large colorful piñata, which spilled candy out all over the ground. The only drawback was that he had been blindfolded. As soon as the piñata burst, all the other children had rushed in and scooped up most of the candy before Carlos could rip off the mask and join them. He had gotten only three pieces of candy, while the other children's hands and pockets were bulging with the sweet treasures.

Still, he was proud of the fact that he had delivered the final blow to the papier-mâché piñata, which was shaped like a giant parrot. All the other children had cheered as he had swung the broom handle. Unfortunately, as soon as the candy was picked up, lightning flashed and thunder rumbled in the distance. During the party, dark clouds had moved across the mountains and over the little seaside town. The party had broken up. Carlos and Julie and several other kids had decided to walk back to the orphanage.

"We can beat the rain," Carlos had told his father and mother. "Besides, even if it does rain, we'll just get a little bit wet. Please, please, please?"

A few moments later, Carlos and the others were climbing up the winding street to the top of the hill. The children had stopped to catch their breath from all the climbing when they heard the scream.

"It came from the church."

"No, from behind the church," Julie said. "From the cemetery."

Now everyone forgot the storm and the party. Each child stared into the darkness. A light flashed behind the old church building among the graves. All the children looked toward the light. Carlos was sure he saw a shadowy shape moving among the old gravestones. The dark clouds overhead made the night that much darker and lonelier. A sudden gust of wind blew dust across the street. Lightning flashed in the distance, followed by a slow rumbling of thunder. But as soon as the thunder stopped, they heard the low wailing scream again.

"What was that?" Carlos asked the others.

"I don't know," Miguel replied. "It sounded awful, like someone could be dying. Maybe it's someone from the graves."

"¡Los muertos, los muertos!" María cried fearfully. "Lo están haciendo otra vez." The nine-year-old girl began to tug at Miguel's hand, pulling her older brother away from the old church. Her dark eyes were fixed on the shadowy graves in the distant cemetery.

Miguel, who was ten and short for his age, stepped between his sister and the graveyard as a protector. The right lens of his glasses was cracked, so he cocked his head slightly so he could see the graves better. He took a deep breath and faced the darkness, trying to act brave yet hoping no one noticed how hard his heart was pounding.

" 'Los muertos'?" Carlos asked, trying to think quickly what the words meant.

" 'The dead people,' " Julie said quickly. "She said, 'They're doing it again.' "

"The dead people are doing what again?" Carlos asked in surprise. "How can dead people do anything, let alone do it again?"

Even though Carlos had been born in Mexico, Julie was the one who knew more Spanish because she liked speaking the language and studied harder than Carlos. When he was very young, his parents had died. Carlos had been adopted by Pastor Brown and his family. He never even knew anything about Mexico until he was five years old and the Browns returned to Santiago to help out the people at the orphanage.

Every year since then, the Springdale Community Church sent a team of people to Santiago to work in the orphanage and in the town of Santiago, which was on the eastern coast of Mexico, north of Veracruz. Carlos and Julie loved being part of the missions trips. There was always lots of hard work, but they enjoyed being in another country.

During that week the young people and adults from Springdale had helped paint the entire orphanage, inside and out. On some days, the young people from the Springdale church had sung in the town plaza and acted out skits in Spanish and English. Earlier that morning, all the other families had begun the trip back home to Springdale, leaving Carlos and his family. Pastor Brown had decided to stay a few more days to help Pastor Pablo. Hearing the strange crying voices made Carlos wish he was safe with the others on their way to the United States. Another wailing noise split the air. Carlos jerked back. Julie shivered.

"Los muertos gritan," María moaned.

" 'The dead people scream,' " Julie translated.

"Dead people don't make sounds." Carlos peered into the shadows behind the old mission. Carlos, who wanted to be a scientist when he got older, always tried to understand things in a logical, scientific manner.

"What about ghosts?" María asked.

"Do ghosts make sounds?" Julie asked with concern.

"I believe in the Holy Ghost, which is another name for the Holy Spirit," Carlos said. "But I don't believe in ghosts that float around and scare people. That voice sounded human."

"It sounded weird to me," Julie said.

"But ghosts are the spirits of dead people, aren't they?" Miguel replied. "It could be a ghost. The kids in the orphanage are talking about ghosts. Some have seen strange things. Others have heard noises."

"Maybe they were dreaming. I haven't heard anyone talk about this before," Carlos said skeptically.

"No one talks about it too much," Miguel said uneasily. "This past week everyone was busy with painting and doing things with their church friends from Springdale. I don't think anyone saw or heard the ghost the whole time."

"I haven't heard Pastor Pablo talk about any ghosts."

"Pastor Pablo doesn't want the little ones to get scared since we all live next door to the old church," Miguel replied.

"But we are scared," María said, choosing her words carefully. She spoke English slowly, trying not to make mistakes. The little girl's large brown eyes returned to the shadowy darkness behind the old church.

The church and the orphanage were at the north end of the town on a small foothill of the mountains overlooking the bay. Most nights you could see the moonlight dancing on the water. But this night was too dark. Carlos could smell the salty sea air as another gust of wind cut through the dark night. He was about to suggest they leave when they heard a noise behind them.

"Woooooo!" a voice yelled. Everyone but Carlos screamed as they turned around. Miguel was already running down the street.

"Flaco!" Julie yelled. "You scared us!"

"I know," laughed a tall skinny boy. He smiled at everyone. Then he reached down to scratch his ankle. His bare feet were dirty. The orphanage provided all the children with shoes, but

Flaco never wore them. "Look at poor Miguel run. He looks like a jackrabbit being chased by a coyote."

"That's not funny, Flaco," María said, her dark eyes flashing. "You shouldn't sneak up on us like that. You know that scares us."

"I was just running after Roberto," Flaco said, still grinning, enjoying the fear he had caused in the others. "He said he was going to catch up with you guys."

"That's a lie," Miguel said. "Roberto isn't with us."

"He told me he was going with you guys," Flaco insisted.

"You're just trying to scare us," María accused. "You always lie or make excuses."

"I do not!" Flaco shot back angrily. "Can I help it if you babies get scared in the dark?"

Carlos didn't say anything. He didn't really like Flaco. In fact, not many of the children in the orphanage liked the tall skinny boy because he often said cruel things or played mean jokes on the others. He had only been at the orphanage six months and hadn't made many friends. Several children had complained about Flaco to Pastor Pablo. Even though he had been in trouble several times with the pastor, once even for stealing, Flaco didn't seem to change his angry ways. Earlier that week, Emily Morgan's portable radio and cassette player had disappeared. No one could prove he had stolen it, but everyone, including Carlos, suspected Flaco. Emily had left that morning without recovering the cassette player.

"Chi chi chi chi," Flaco said, flapping his arms like a bird. He laughed and pointed to Miguel.

"We aren't scared," Miguel shot back as he returned to the group. He bent down to pick his glasses off the street. He wiped the lenses with his shirt and put them back on.

"You ran like the little bird you are," Flaco replied with a smug smile. "You ran so fast you left your glasses behind."

"You be quiet," Miguel said fiercely.

"Are you going to fight me?" Flaco asked angrily. He made his hands into fists as he stepped toward Miguel. He towered over the smaller boy. Miguel looked mad enough to fight, but he knew he wouldn't have a chance. He took a step backwards and looked down at the ground in shame. His glasses slipped on his nose, and he grabbed them to prevent them from falling off.

"See, you are a little chicken, a *pollito*," Flaco said with disgust. Then he turned to Carlos. "Do you want to fight with me?"

"I'm not looking for a fight," Carlos said. He was ten, and though he was average size for his age, Flaco was still much taller. Carlos burned with anger and frustration at the larger boy's taunts and teases.

"Are you a little *pollito* too?" Flaco asked, smiling his smug smile.

"Carlos isn't afraid of you," Julie said hotly.

"So your big sister will fight for you?" Flaco said. "Is that how they do it in the United States? The sisters fight for their *pollito* brothers?"

"Quit calling me a *pollito*," Carlos replied. He took a step toward the older boy.

"What are you going to do about it?" Flaco demanded. "Maybe I should ask your sister. She's the fighter in the family."

"I'm not afraid of big mouths like you," Carlos said, standing up straighter. Flaco smiled.

The tall, skinny boy was about to make a reply when it

happened. A gust of wind shook the leaves in the trees, and an eerie green light flashed in the darkness among the gravestones. All the children saw the light briefly before it was smothered by the darkness.

"You saw that, didn't you?" Miguel asked, his lips quivering. He shifted his head slightly to see better through his broken glasses.

"¡Los muertos!" María shuddered.

"I think we should get out of here," Julie said nervously.

"Maybe," Carlos said, still staring into the darkness.

Flaco looked surprised and then scared. The older boy stared fearfully at the darkness. He looked back at the others. His whole attitude had changed.

"It *is* true," Flaco said softly. "I thought the other kids were scared or making up stories."

"They were scared for a reason," Miguel replied.

"We better get back to the orphanage," Carlos said.

"But the ghost is near the fence!" Flaco said. "We'd have to walk right by it!"

"That's the only way," Carlos insisted. He took a few steps up the road toward the church and graveyard. His feet were the only ones making sounds. He turned and looked around. Julie and the others stood together in a tight little group, as if their feet were planted in the road. Even Flaco was standing as close as he could get to the other children.

"Come on," Carlos said. "Let's get home before—"

"Ooooooooooiiiiiiiieeeeeee!" a voice cried out in the darkness. Carlos whirled around. The eerie green glowing figure was closer. This time they could see it more clearly. The vaguely human shape stood right at the old broken iron gate of the cemetery. Carlos looked and blinked his eyes. Where there should have been feet there was just darkness. The ghost appeared to be floating two feet above the ground. When it passed through the half-open gate and came closer, Carlos had seen enough.

Screams filled the air. Carlos turned around to run. The others were already speeding down the road as fast as they could go, shrieking at the top of their lungs. Carlos didn't look back. He ran as fast as he could go and caught up with the group. None of them stopped running until they reached the plaza in town. They stopped by the little fountain in the center of the plaza.

The wind blew harder. All the people at the birthday party were gone. The whole plaza was deserted. Everything looked dark and lonely. A few drops of rain began to fall on the dusty brown cobblestones. Miguel, who had been carrying his glasses while he ran, turned his face away from the others and put the glasses back on. He didn't want any more teasing from Flaco.

"Where will we go?" Julie panted, trying to catch her breath. "Everything looks closed up."

"I don't know," Carlos replied. He looked behind him up the street. There was no sign of the ghost. Suddenly, another boy came down the road and streaked across the plaza after them. As he came closer, everyone recognized the large lumbering figure by his awkward run.

"Roberto!" Miguel yelled. "Did you see it too?"

Roberto ran flat footed over to the group of children. He was almost as tall as Flaco, yet he had a large, heavyset body with stooped shoulders. The boy's round face was sweaty. Like the others he was out of breath. His black hair was shaved on the sides and cut flat and short on the top like a soldier's.

He looked over his shoulder several times.

"A ghost was at the old church!" Roberto panted.

"We know!" María said.

"I was coming up the hill," Roberto said. "I saw you run by me. Then I saw the ghost coming down the street after you. I was afraid and ran too."

"What if it comes into the plaza?" Miguel asked.

"We need to get out of here," Flaco said uneasily.

"But where will we go?" María cried. Everyone looked back up the street they had come down.

"Let's go to Señora Garza's," Roberto said. "Her store will still be open."

The children ran across the plaza as fast as they could go. Señora Garza had the largest bodega in town. The children opened the door to the shop just as the rain began to fall harder.

Everyone rushed inside the store. Carlos was the last person in. He didn't feel totally safe until the door was shut behind him. The other children crowded up to the small window at the front of the store and looked past the decorative iron bars out into the plaza. There was no sign of the ghost.

Carlos turned around. Señora Garza's store was much bigger on the inside than it appeared from the plaza. It reminded him of the convenience stores back in Springdale. On the far end by the door were tables and chairs where people could sit down to eat and drink and talk. Señora Garza's store was part cantina, part grocery and part dry goods store. She seemed to have a little bit of everything in the store. There were cases of sodas, candy, potato chips, canned goods, coffee beans, stacks of bananas, mangos and other fruits, big containers of dried beans and rice, mops and brooms, brightly colored blankets, magazines, ceramic figures, motor oil, coils of rope and string, electrical cords, and even some toys like kites and balls. One shelf was filled with firecrackers and an odd assortment of fireworks. Strung across the ceiling of the store on a long wire were dozens of papier-mâché piñatas. A bright piñata of a parrot, exactly like the one at the birthday party earlier, was the prettiest.

All the tables were occupied. Señora Garza also sold sandwiches and drinks and pastries. Some old women sat at one table, drinking coffee. At another were a man and his wife and their children eating sandwiches called tortas and drinking sodas from bottles. At another table some men were playing cards and drinking beer from dark brown bottles.

"¡Niños!" a large woman with a big smile said. A blue and red scarf was wrapped around her dark hair. She wore a loose, brightly colored dress that resembled a kimono. "Is the birthday party over? I hope the rain did not spoil things."

"We're trying to escape the ghost!" Roberto said. The big boy pointed out toward the plaza. He wiped his face, which was still sweating.

"Ghost?" Señora Garza asked with surprise.

"Sí, tenemos mucho miedo," María said. Carlos caught part of the words, like *los muertos*. Then the others began talking all at once. The adults at the tables began to listen to the children. The women drinking coffee began to frown and talk fearfully together. Soon, the whole store was filled with voices, each trying to be heard above the others.

"So we ran back down the hill into the plaza," Julie said to the big woman. "Roberto said he saw it coming down the street after us, but we didn't see it come into the plaza."

One of the old women had left her table and was looking out into the plaza. She shook her head at the other old women.

Carlos could tell they seemed to be afraid of the ghost.

"I've heard stories about that old church for years," Señora Garza said loudly so all the others in the café could hear. "That church was abandoned many years ago after a horrible earthquake. They said it was not safe to go back inside it. In fact, some people said a priest was swallowed up by the ground at the old church. Maybe it's his ghost you saw. Nothing would surprise me. Some people say they've seen that ghost around the orphanage itself. I hope the children are safe . . ."

The men and women began to talk rapidly, nodding. All of them remembered the earthquake because it was the biggest in the town's history.

"I bet it's his ghost," Roberto said to the other children. "I bet the whole church is haunted. Don't you think so? Maybe it's not safe to be in the orphanage. Maybe it's too close to the old church. What if the ghost goes to the orphanage?"

"I don't think we should jump to conclusions," Carlos said.

"But you saw it," Flaco said. "We all saw it."

"We all saw something," Carlos said slowly. "And I was scared just like you. But it was awfully dark. We saw some kind of light. I just don't believe—"

The sudden sound of a siren cut off the boy's words. Everyone ran to the window to look, but then it was too crowded. Señora Garza opened the door so they could all see out into the plaza. A police car sped around the corner, its red light flashing and siren blaring. It sped across the plaza and started up the road that led to the old church and orphanage. Everyone watched until the car drove out of sight.

"Maybe others have seen the ghost too," Señora Garza said solemnly to the whole room. "Or maybe the ghost caught a child who didn't run as fast as you children."

The old men and women in the bodega began murmuring, considering Señora Garza's words. One or two made the Sign of the Cross. María crept closer to Miguel, her lower lip trembling. Carlos felt himself shivering as a gust of cold damp air blew through the doorway. He and the others listened to the wail of the siren as it got fainter and fainter, lost in the falling rain and rumbling thunder.

Chapter Two

When They Prayed

The bodega was filled with anxious voices talking about ghosts, the police car and the big earthquake that had shaken the old church. Carlos and Julie stood by the window looking out at the rain hitting the cobblestones in the plaza. Miguel and María walked over to them.

"We should be back at the orphanage," Julie said finally.

"I wonder if they're worried about us," Carlos asked.

"Maybe. They probably think we got caught in the rain."

"What about the ghost?" Carlos asked.

"How would they know about that?"

Carlos shrugged. "I guess they wouldn't."

"Many of the children in the orphanage have been talking about ghosts," María informed the others.

"I never heard anyone mention ghosts before tonight," Julie said.

"The week before several of the kids in the orphanage were talking about ghosts," Miguel said. "Some said they saw strange things. Others heard weird noises."

"But we are scared," María added. The little girl's large brown eyes revealed her fear. "I was hoping the ghost had gone away. All the kids were hoping the ghost left."

"I was hoping it had left too," Miguel said. "Then tonight—"

Just then, the door blew open and a tall man with a big black mustache walked in. The big mustache was dripping water. His black hair was shiny and wet. But he didn't even seem to notice he was so wet. He looked quickly around the room. When he saw Señora Garza standing behind the counter, he walked over to her. The smile disappeared from Señora Garza's face as the tall man approached. He began talking rapidly. Even from across the room, the children could tell by his tone of voice that he was unhappy about something. Señora Garza listened and drew him further behind the counter so others wouldn't hear.

"That's Señor Gómez," Miguel reported to the others.

"Isn't his store on the opposite side of the plaza?" Carlos asked.

"He has the second biggest store in town," Miguel said. "Señora Garza's store is bigger."

"Señor Gómez doesn't like Señora Garza," María added. "Señor Gómez is jealous, people say, because his store is smaller. Plus Señora Garza has other businesses that make much more money. She sells things at the border."

"What does she sell?" Carlos asked.

"Things the tourists buy," Miguel said. "She sells stuff like blankets, handmade dolls, piñatas and some little ceramic bulls. She makes much money. Her house is very big."

"Where does she get the things she sells?" Carlos asked.

"From around here," Miguel said. "In the little towns in the mountains around here the people make things. She buys them and sends them by truck to the border. The people in town say she has a very good business."

"Señor Gómez is just jealous because of her good fortune," María said. "She treats us very kind. Last Christmas she brought presents to the orphanage."

Carlos observed Señor Gómez carefully. Although the man spoke angrily, wagging his finger at the large woman, Señora Garza didn't seem upset. Flaco leaned with his back against the counter near Señora Garza and her angry competitor. Señor Gómez suddenly stopped talking and spoke harshly to Flaco. The boy moved away and sat on top of a case of empty soda bottles.

Carlos opened the door of the bodega. Miguel and the others crowded up around him. Carlos stepped outside just far enough not to get wet. The wind was blowing from behind the building so there was a space of about a foot and a half that was protected from the falling rain.

"Oye! Pssssttt!" someone whispered harshly.

"What?" Carlos asked. He turned in the direction of the sound. Two men covered with wet cloth ponchos stood at the corner of the building. They both looked dirty and poor. One had a blue patch over his eye. The one with the patch motioned for Carlos to come talk.

"Some guys out here want to talk to me," Carlos whispered to the others. Miguel and María stuck their heads out the door. The two men walked slowly in front of the building. The man without the patch limped. They looked in the front window of the bodega carefully and then went closer to the door. Carlos stepped back, unsure of their motives.

"¿Qué quieren?" Miguel asked as the men came closer. "What do you want?"

The man with the patch began to whisper, too fast for Carlos to catch many of the words. Señor Limp suddenly grabbed Señor Patch Eye's shoulder. He looked through the window and immediately stopped speaking. Both men turned and ran down the side of the building and around the corner.

"What in the world was he so upset about?" Carlos turned to ask his friends. Miguel and María had moved aside as Señor Gómez stepped through the door, followed by Señora Garza. The tall man glared back at the woman and looked suspiciously at Carlos and the others. He still seemed angry as he walked out into the rainy night. He crossed the plaza toward his own store.

"Come inside, children, before you get wet," Señora Garza said. "I will take you back to the orphanage so no one will worry that the ghost got you."

"The ghost?" Carlos asked. For a moment Carlos had forgotten about what they had seen at the church.

"Wait here by the door, and I will get my car," Señora Garza said with a smile. The large woman walked across the floor. She said something to another man sitting behind the counter.

"That's Señora Garza's brother," Miguel said. "He runs the store when she is away on business."

"I wondered who he was," Julie said. "Uh, oh, here comes Flaco."

The boy got up and walked over to the children standing by the door. He smiled. When no one smiled back, he looked angry. Roberto stared at Flaco suspiciously. Flaco walked a few feet away from the others.

"Who were those two men outside?" Carlos demanded. "And what were they saying? Why did they run away like that?"

"I don't know their names," Miguel said solemnly. "But I've seen them at our church services. They were there several weeks ago."

"That's great," Julie said. "But why were they acting so odd?"

"They were afraid," María said. "They said for us to be careful."

"Be careful?" Carlos repeated. "But why?"

"Señor Patch Eye said the orphanage was in danger," Miguel replied.

"Who said the orphanage was in danger?" Roberto asked as he joined the others. The big boy stooped down so he could listen to the younger children. Carlos quickly told him about the two men in front of the store.

"Is that all he said?" Roberto asked.

"I think so," Miguel said. "He sure seemed afraid of something. He ran away when Señor Gómez came to the door."

"I've seen those men before," Roberto said and frowned. "I wouldn't trust them. They're just drunks and bums. They'd say anything so you'd give them money."

"They didn't ask for money," Miguel replied.

"They would have if they had stayed longer," Roberto said. "I'm sure I've seen those men begging before."

"But Miguel said they'd been to church a few weeks ago," Julie said. "Maybe they changed. Maybe they know something we don't. Maybe the orphanage is really in some kind of danger."

A car horn honked as a big black Cadillac rolled in front of the store. Señora Garza smiled and waved for the children to get inside. She pulled as close to the building as possible. Miguel got in first, followed by the others.

"Wait!" Julie said as Carlos was about to close the door. Flaco stood in the doorway. It was obvious that he wanted a ride too. Carlos waited until the tall thin boy got in the car beside him.

"Thanks, gringo," Flaco said.

"His name is Carlos," Roberto said.

"Thank you, Carlos," Flaco said sarcastically. He stared at Roberto in anger. Flaco and Roberto often argued. They had plenty of opportunity because they shared a room at the orphanage. The car was uncomfortably quiet as Señora Garza drove up the hill to the orphanage. Carlos and the others looked intently out the windows as the car passed the old church, but no one saw anything unusual. However, up ahead by the orphanage, a flashing red light pulsed in the night.

"Looks like trouble," Carlos said as they drove closer. As they rounded the curve, they all saw the red light flashing across the front of the orphanage.

"That doesn't look good," Julie said softly.

"I wonder what's wrong?" María said fearfully.

"I hope it's not the ghost," Señora Garza said slowly. "This is a bad sign."

She drove the big black car up next to the police car. The children ran from the car through the rain to the front door of the orphanage. The big main room, which served as a dining hall and assembly room, was filled with people. Mrs. Brown looked relieved when she saw Julie and Carlos.

"Are you two all right?" Mrs. Brown asked. "You don't feel sick?"

"I feel fine," Julie replied as her mother reached over to touch her forehead. "What's wrong?"

"Your father left a few minutes ago with Pastor Pablo and three other children," Mrs. Brown said, her voice cracking. Her eyes filled with tears.

"What's wrong, Mom?" Carlos began to feel afraid. He immediately thought of the ghost.

"No one is sure what happened," Mrs. Brown said. "Pastor Pablo and the four children, Lucita, Jorge, Ricardo and Isabel, left the party in his car. They dropped off little Lucita at her home in town and then came here. They were helping him in his office, when they became very sick."

"Sick?"

"Very sick." Mrs. Brown wiped a tear from her eye. "The children began passing out. One vomited. Then Pastor Pablo lost consciousness too. Your father and Señor Losada called the police. By the time the police got here, they were worse. Your father and the police chief, Señor Vega, decided to use the van owned by the orphanage and take all four of them to the hospital in Veracruz."

"There's no ambulance?" Julie asked.

"Santiago is lucky to even have a police car," Mrs. Brown said. "It's too small a town to have an ambulance too. The quickest way to get them to the hospital was to use the orphanage van."

"They'll be okay, won't they?" Carlos asked.

"I don't know," Mrs. Brown said. "We all need to be praying very hard. In fact, why don't you two get some of the older ones and gather them to pray? That will help the younger children. Everyone is very scared right now. We really need God's help. I've got to try and make some phone calls."

Mrs. Brown hurried away. Señora Garza stood in the corner talking to the deputy police chief. The children were huddled in small groups. Carlos and Julie found Miguel and María. By then they had heard about Pastor Pablo and the others being rushed to the hospital.

"Gather up all the children and let's meet by the stage to pray," Julie instructed the others. "Carlos, you go check the dorm rooms and bring back anyone you find so we can all pray together."

There were almost seventy children in the orphanage. Most of them were in the big meeting hall talking about the sick children and Pastor Pablo. Julie, Miguel and María moved through the big hall, gathering them together.

Carlos ran through the big kitchen, past the pantry and out the side door. The big dormitory hall stood right next to the dining hall. Half of the dormitory held rooms for girls and the other half housed the boys. Carlos found only two boys in one of the rooms. He shouted down the girls' side of the dormitory. A single girl came out of her room. Carlos told her to check the other rooms and then to come to the dining hall.

While she was checking the rooms, Carlos ran back outside. The rain had let up for a moment. He didn't see any other children. He ducked into the kitchen and was headed toward the big meeting room when he saw Flaco coming out of the food pantry closet. The tall thin boy looked surprised at being discovered. None of the children were supposed to be in the pantry. It was a kitchen rule. Carlos knew about it. But Flaco's hands looked empty.

"We're all meeting in the big hall to pray," Carlos said.

"So what?" Flaco said.

"But we're going to pray for Pastor Pablo," Carlos said. "Didn't you hear about what happened?"

"I heard," Flaco said brusquely.

"Well, are you going to pray with us?"

"Leave me alone," Flaco shot back. "You aren't my boss."

"I'm not trying to be your boss." Carlos tried to control his anger. He wanted to say something else, but decided against it. Flaco walked away without looking back. Carlos ran back into the meeting room.

It looked like almost all the children were by the stage at the front of the big room. Some sat in chairs, other stood up and others were on the floor, heads bowed. They had already started praying. Señora Garza and the deputy police officer were talking to Mrs. Brown and Señor Losada by the open front door. Then the deputy and Señora Garza left.

Carlos joined the other children in praying. Most of the prayers were in Spanish. Carlos had to concentrate very hard, and even then he didn't understand much since many of the children spoke so softly.

But he could hear the love and concern in their voices. Pastor Pablo was like a father to many of the children. He had founded the orphanage and kept it going for over ten years. Carlos wondered if the orphanage could survive without Pastor Pablo. Apparently some of the children were wondering the same thing.

They had prayed for twenty minutes. Carlos felt a change in the air. It was somehow lighter as prayer pushed out worry and brought peace. Suddenly, a bright flash of lightning lit up the room. A few seconds later, a clap of thunder shook the whole building. Several children cried out in surprise. Everyone's eyes opened. A few children laughed. The ones nearest the windows began moving toward the center of the room.

Lightning flashed again. Then the lights suddenly went out. As darkness covered the room, thunder shook the building again. In the darkness, children began to talk.

"I'll go to the kitchen and get the flashlights," Mrs. Brown announced. But before she could take two steps, a wail split the air.

"¡Los muertos! ¡Los muertos!" somebody cried out. Carlos jumped in fear. Like everyone else, his eye was drawn to the eerie green light right outside the closest window. A ghostly figure with two dark places for eyes and a dark place for a mouth was right outside the glass.

Screams filled the air. Children panicked and ran from the window. Some children fell and others tripped over them in the darkness. The noises grew louder. The eerie green presence hung at the window for a few seconds more and then suddenly disappeared. The room was dark once more.

Chapter Three

Carlos Investigates

I was never so glad to get through a single night in my life." Carlos was eating breakfast the next morning in the big meeting room that was set up as a dining hall. Several long tables were arranged in rows. The children ate scrambled eggs, beans and rice with hot corn tortillas and butter. The food was filling, but Carlos was tired of beans and rice, since they ate those with almost every meal.

"I barely slept," Julie added. "All the girls wanted to sleep in our room. It was wall-to-wall people, and they kept talking and wouldn't go to sleep."

"Who could blame them?" Miguel asked. The small boy picked at his food. "After seeing the ghost at the window, I didn't think I would go to sleep myself. I was too scared it would come to my room."

"I don't believe in any ghosts," Carlos said. "It's not logical."

"But you saw it," María said. "You saw it twice."

"I saw something," Carlos said carefully. "But I don't believe it was a ghost."

"What was it then?" Miguel asked.

"I don't know for sure," Carlos said. "But it's too coincidental. The lights go out and then minutes later this ghost appears."

"But the storm caused the lights to go out, didn't it?" Roberto asked.

"I wouldn't be so sure," Carlos said. "Señor Losada said the main breaker was off. I don't think lightning would trip the main breaker because the lightning didn't strike near us. If you remember, the thunder came several seconds after we saw the lightning, which was south of here. In fact it would have been south of the whole town. But when Señor Losada and I went outside last night, the lights in town seemed to be on. So our lights should have been on too."

"Everyone thinks the storm turned off the lights," Roberto said between bites. The large boy eagerly wolfed down the last of his food. "It's happened before."

"Maybe the ghost turned off the lights," Flaco said from the next table over. The boy was eating by himself.

"What do you know about it?" Miguel demanded.

"How would you know anything?" Roberto added. "You get the worst grades in school."

"I know more than you think," Flaco said with a thin, hard smile. He ate the last bite of a tortilla and stood up. He carried his tray toward the kitchen without saying anything else.

"I don't trust him," Roberto said softly. "He's a thief. I bet he took Emily's cassette player."

"You really shouldn't accuse people without facts," Julie said.

"But he's the kind of boy that would take it," Miguel said. "He was caught stealing before. I don't like him. He's always ready to pick a fight."

"At least you don't have to have him stay in your room like me," Roberto said. The large boy scratched his ear. "I've asked Pastor Pablo to move him out of my room many times, but he won't do it. But someday soon I will go to live with a nice family, and I will have my own room. I won't have to share with Flaco or anyone else ever again."

"Have you heard that someone wants you to live with them?" Miguel asked enviously.

"I know it will happen," Roberto said confidently. The big boy ran his hand nervously over the flat top of his hair.

"But how can you be so sure?" Miguel asked. "Pastor Pablo never tells any of the children until a day or two before they leave."

"Maybe I know something Pastor Pablo doesn't know," Roberto replied sharply. He looked at the others defiantly, as if daring them to doubt his words. But it was too early in the morning for an argument. The table was quiet for a moment.

"I wonder how Pastor Pablo is doing," María said.

"Not very well," Julie said. "My father called here last night. He didn't give many details, but he said they're all very sick. They're running tests. They think it may be something they ate. He stayed at the hospital all night and is still there. He must really be tired."

"Maybe it's something they ate at the party," Carlos said.

"That's what mother thought too," Julie replied. "But we all had the same cake and drinks. No one else is sick."

"You're right," Carlos said. "I wonder what it could be then."

"Will you go back to Springdale on Monday like you planned?" María asked.

"I don't know," Julie said. "My mother said we may be here longer since Pastor Pablo is so sick. She's glad we decided to stay the few extra days now."

"Good," Carlos said. "I want to investigate this whole matter. I wish the other Home School Detectives could have stayed down here to help me."

"Who are the Home School Detectives?" Miguel asked. He shifted his head to one side to see through the cracked lens of his glasses. Carlos tried hard not to stare at the broken lens. The lens had broken earlier that week and would take another week to replace. He knew the small boy was self-conscious about the way he looked in the broken glasses.

"Julie and I, and our friends, Josh and Emily Morgan, and Billy and Rebecca Renner," Carlos said proudly.

"They left yesterday," María said.

"Back home, we've solved mysteries just as hard as this. We've helped the police and everything," Carlos said.

"We need to put our detective hats on to figure all this stuff out," Julie said.

"You really solve mysteries?" Roberto asked with surprise.

"We sure try," Carlos said. "And that's just what I'm going to do today. We're done with all the painting. And we've completed all the schoolwork we brought along. I want to take some time to investigate."

"Can I help?" Miguel asked. "Can someone like me be a detective too?"

"Sure," Carlos said confidently. He wanted to be a scientist when he got older and always tried to understand things in a logical, scientific manner. "Being a detective is a lot like doing research for school projects. You ask obvious questions and see where the answers lead."

"Where will you start?" Miguel asked.

"Follow me." Carlos carried his tray over to a side table by the kitchen door. The others followed. They left the trays in a stack and put the silverware in a tub of sudsy water.

"I'll see you all later," Julie said. "I told Mom I would help her this morning."

Carlos went outside. Miguel and Roberto followed him. Carlos walked around the big meeting hall to the window where the ghost had appeared the night before. Carlos studied the window and the dark red muddy ground.

"What are you looking for?"

"Evidence."

"What kind of evidence?" Roberto asked. "Ghosts don't leave evidence."

"Maybe they do," Carlos said. He bent down and looked carefully at the red mud. Two bare feet walked into view. Carlos looked up. The bare feet belonged to Flaco.

"I thought maybe there would be footprints," Carlos said.

"Footprints of a ghost?" Flaco asked. "You should try to find footprints in the wind."

"He's right for once," Roberto agreed. "Ghosts don't leave footprints. They float through walls and fly through the air."

"Maybe." Carlos was still thinking. "But I'm going to keep investigating. I'm going to the church."

"This is all foolishness," Roberto said. "You are wasting your time chasing around after ghosts. I'll see you later."

Roberto walked back around the building. Miguel shrugged his shoulders. Flaco watched Roberto leave.

"Let's go to the church and graveyard," Carlos said.

"Not me." Flaco walked away. Carlos was almost glad to see the moody boy leave.

"I guess it's just you and me," Carlos said to Miguel. "Let's go."

The two boys walked down the road to the old church and graveyard. In daylight the church didn't seem nearly as spooky. Carlos walked past the old, crumbling adobe walls and headed straight for the graveyard. He stopped at the broken gate and began examining the ground.

The red dirt was muddy but smooth. Carlos was plainly disappointed.

"Any footprints would have been washed away by the storm," Carlos said. "That's probably what happened outside the window too."

"If there were footprints," Miguel said.

"Wait a minute," Carlos said. "Look at the weeds."

He pointed inside the gate. Knee-high weeds filled the graveyard, half-covering the old white tombstones.

"The weeds are bent," Carlos said excitedly. "Don't you see? Someone could have been walking there and bent them like that."

"Maybe," Miguel replied skeptically. "They just look wet and beaten down from the rain. The storm could do that."

Carlos bent closer to the grass. He pulled at a clump of the tall grass carefully. He examined another clump and then another.

"Look how some of these grass stems are broken close to the ground," Carlos said. He pointed at the grass stems so Miguel could see them more clearly. The small boy nodded as he pushed his glasses up higher on his nose. Something had broken the stems. "The rain would flatten the weeds, but these weeds are broken. They were dry when they were stepped on. It hadn't rained yet last night when we saw the ghost, remember?"

Carlos moved inside the graveyard and walked toward one of the graves. Then he walked back, examining his path. He smiled and bent over to look where he had just walked. He examined his own footprints in the weeds.

"These grass stems where I walked are bent but not broken in the same way as those others," Carlos said. Miguel nodded. "Someone was walking here before it rained."

"Maybe someone was walking through here, but that doesn't mean it was the ghost," Miguel said.

"You're right about that," Carlos said. "But it does prove someone was walking here in the same place where we saw the ghost. That's possible evidence."

Carlos looked at the ground around the gate once more. As he started back out to the road, his leg caught on a dangling iron bar on the broken gate. His pant leg would have torn if he had kept going. Carlos carefully pulled his blue jeans free. As he did, he stopped. He reached down and picked up a few thick black threads off the sharp piece of iron.

"Someone has been through here before," Carlos said, holding up the threads. Miguel nodded with admiration.

"Someone wore a black pair of pants or a skirt or something," Miguel said. "But that doesn't mean it was a ghost. And those threads could have been there a long time."

"You're right again," Carlos said. "But it's still something to think about. Let's take a look inside the old church."

"I don't want to go in there," Miguel said.

"But we need to look around," Carlos insisted and began walking toward the front of the old church.

"But they say it's not safe in there since the earthquake,"

Miguel replied as he followed his friend out into the street.

"We'll just look inside the doorway." Carlos walked up the street to the front of the church. He went up the worn cement steps carefully. He stepped inside the old door of the church. Most of the roof had fallen in, and the old building was well lit by daylight. Miguel stepped in behind his friend. Carlos took a few steps inside. The room was large. Pieces of fallen roof were in the middle of the floor along with a piece of a white candle. Several green vines were growing up out of the floor and on the walls.

"There's nothing in here," Miguel said nervously.

"Wait," Carlos said. He pulled Miguel closer to the wall. Outside, they could hear voices. Carlos peeked around the edge of the doorway.

"It's Flaco," Carlos whispered.

Miguel peeked outside too. The tall skinny boy with no shoes was standing in the street near the front of the old church. The boy looked around in all directions, as if to see if anyone was watching. He looked over at the graveyard carefully. Two men came into view as they walked up the street. One wore an eye patch and the other walked with a limp.

"It's the two men from last night who were acting so secretive and scared," Carlos whispered. "It looks like they know Flaco."

Mr. Limp began talking to Flaco. The tall boy listened and nodded his head.

"What are they saying? What are they saying?" Carlos whispered to Miguel.

"Sssshhhhh!" The small boy listened. The men turned around and headed down the hill. Flaco walked down the hill with them.

"What did they say?"

"I couldn't hear very well," Miguel said. "They did mention the ghost. And they were saying something about the docks."

"The docks?" Carlos asked.

"I think they are going into town to the docks where all the fishing boats stay," Miguel replied. "They wanted Flaco to go with them."

"This may be the break we're looking for," Carlos said excitedly.

"What break?" Miguel asked.

"We've got to follow them," Carlos said with determination. "Quick, before we lose sight of them!"

The two boys slipped out of the church building. Carlos ran down the old steps. When he reached the street, Flaco and the two men had disappeared.

"Where'd they go?" Miguel asked in surprise.

"I don't know," Carlos said. "They just vanished."

"Just like ghosts," the smaller boy said. Carlos looked down the empty street and nodded.

Chapter Four

At the Dock

I know those two men said something about the docks to Flaco," Miguel said.

"If we hurry, maybe we'll see them in the plaza," Carlos said.

"I don't know," Miguel said doubtfully.

Carlos began to run. Going down the cobblestone street reminded Carlos of running away from the ghost the night before. This time he wasn't scared of a ghost. He was more afraid that he wouldn't be able to follow Flaco.

The town of Santiago looked exceptionally clean as the boys ran into the plaza. Before the rain, everything had been dusty and dingy. Now the leaves of plants looked shiny and fresh. The cars parked on the street looked clean. Even the stucco and stone buildings looked fresh. Some of the cobblestones were still wet and shiny in the morning sun.

"I think I just saw them over by the market." Miguel

pointed. Carlos looked.

"I don't see them," Carlos said.

"I wasn't sure it was them," Miguel said.

"The docks are down at the end of the market street, aren't they?" Carlos asked. His friend nodded. "Let's go. I don't want them to see us."

"There's too many people for them to notice us in the market," his small friend replied.

Carlos hurried toward the outdoor market, or mercado, as the local people called it. The big outdoor market was south of the main plaza. He loved the market because of the rich smells and unusual sights. Almost everything you could imagine was sold along the street: bright flowers, pots and pans, shoes, cloth in big rolls, clothes, woven baskets and mats, silver and turquoise jewelry, simple wooden furniture, and ceramics.

The market was filled with people. As soon as they started down the street, Carlos realized that it was unlikely that anyone would notice two boys in the crowded street.

"Twenty pesos, twenty pesos!" a man shouted, holding up a large cooking pot he was selling.

"Ten pesos, no more!" an old woman shouted back. Everyone knew that you never paid full price in the market. You bargained and haggled.

"But it's worth fifteen pesos," the man countered. "That's the best price in all of Mexico."

Carlos kept moving down the street. He jumped to one side as a burro covered with bright blankets almost stepped on his feet. As he jumped, his head hit something hard. Stalks of bright green bananas hung from a wire across the street.

"Careful!" a man shouted at Carlos.

"Sorry," Carlos said. A woman with a baby on her back was feeling the bananas. The baby began to cry but the woman didn't seem to notice. The air was filled with the smells of flowers and fruit and vegetables. A man pushing a big wheelbarrow full of potatoes stopped to talk to another man in the middle of the street.

The smells in the air weren't nearly as delightful as the boys entered the part of the market selling meat. Huge red carcasses hung on hooks from wires above his head. The head of a sheep was still attached to one of the bloody carcasses. Flies buzzed and crawled over the exposed meat. The vendor wore a white apron covered with bright bloodstains. He was carving a huge side of beef on a big table. His long sharp knives flashed in his hands as he sliced off hunks of meat.

"I wouldn't eat that, would you?" Carlos said, pointing at an unrecognizable pile of pale meat.

"It's the stomach of a cow," Miguel said simply. "It's kind of chewy."

"Yuck!" Carlos said.

In the next booth, an old woman sat next to a large pot of boiling water. She quickly plucked the feathers off a steaming wet chicken that she had just pulled out of the pot. Another chicken squawked as a man carried it by the legs to the rear of the booth to slaughter it. Carlos didn't want to watch.

He smelled the fish before he saw them. The vendors selling fish were at the end of the street near the docks. There were over two dozen kinds of fish, like shark and redfish, tuna and snapper. Some fish, like the big tunas, were longer than five feet. Others were about the size of sardines.

Several pans were filled with clams, mussels, shrimp and crabs. Carlos reached down into a bushel basket of wet crabs.

Several claws suddenly reached up toward his finger.

"Watch it!" Miguel warned.

"I thought they were dead," Carlos replied. The bony legs clicked as the crabs rearranged themselves in the basket.

The market came to a dead end at the street that ran in front of the docks. Beyond the docks, the blue bay stretched to the horizon. Sparkling sunlight bounced off the small waves.

Both boys walked slowly down the cobblestone street by the edge of the water. The smell of the salty sea was strong. Gentle waves rolled up on shore. The waves in the bay were never very large except in bad storms. A large dead fish had washed up on the shore. Flies covered the bloated fish, and it smelled so bad the boys covered their noses.

"I don't see Flaco," Carlos said, looking up and down the street.

"I don't see his friends either," Miguel replied. "All the fishing boats are gone for the day."

"There's one boat left," Carlos said, pointing to the end of the dock.

"I don't think it's a fishing boat," Miguel told Carlos.

"How can you tell?" Carlos asked.

"It has no nets or arms for nets like the big fishing boats," Miguel replied.

A large truck was backed up to the dock near the boat. Carlos and Miguel walked up to the front of the truck. No one was in sight. They crept along to the rear of the truck. Carlos looked inside. Large brown burlap sacks filled the back of the truck.

"Café," Carlos said, pointing to the word stenciled on the side of a burlap sack.

"That's a lot of coffee." Miguel looked at the sacks.

"I think we lost them," Carlos said with disgust.

"I thought for sure they said they were coming down here," Miguel replied.

"Maybe they were coming down here later in the day," Carlos said.

"Maybe." The smaller boy pushed his glasses up on his nose. "I must not be a very good detective."

"You're a big help," Carlos said, not wanting his friend to feel bad. "We should have followed them more closely, that's all."

Just then, they heard footsteps. Someone was walking down the side of the truck. Carlos quickly motioned for Miguel to follow him. He stepped around to the opposite side of the truck and crouched down behind the big double tires. They looked underneath the truck. From there they saw a pair of pants standing where the two boys just had been. They held their breath until the person walked away from them.

Carlos and Miguel watched. As the man got closer to the boat, they could see his back but not his face. Then he walked up the gangplank to the boat dock.

"It's Señor Gómez," Miguel said.

"Yeah, I wonder what he's doing here," Carlos replied. "I thought it might be those men with Flaco."

Señor Gómez shouted. A man walked out of the cabin on the boat. He looked like he hadn't shaved for a week. His clothes were dirty. He held a beer bottle in his hand. Señor Gómez spoke with the man.

"I can't understand what they're saying," Miguel said.

"Señor Gómez doesn't look too happy," Carlos said. Miguel nodded. The tall store owner talked and wagged his finger at the man with the beer bottle. The man with the beer bottle shrugged and walked back inside the cabin. Señor Gómez stomped down the gangplank. His face was one big scowl, and his big black mustache twitched as he muttered to himself.

"He looked upset." Carlos watched the man head back toward town.

"Señor Gómez worries about too many things," Miguel replied.

Carlos was about to move closer when another man walked out from the cabin on the boat. He strode across the deck of the boat toward the truck. A large dark beard covered his face. His hair was quite long. He wore a red and white striped shirt, and had a rope tied around his waist instead of a belt. Then Carlos noticed the gun. He pulled Miguel down behind the hood of the truck.

"Look, he has a pistol," Carlos whispered. Miguel peeked over the hood of the truck. A black-handled revolver was stuck inside the front of the man's pants. The man scanned the harbor and then walked over to the railing. He spat into the water and reentered the cabin.

"It looks like we're not the only ones interested in the boat," Miguel replied.

"What do you mean?" Carlos asked. His friend pointed back at the boat. They saw a familiar figure in bare feet come from behind the cabin.

"Flaco!" Carlos whispered.

"What's he doing?" Miguel asked.

"It looks like he's sneaking off the boat," Carlos said. The tall boy watched the cabin warily and then tiptoed across the deck. He hurried down the gangplank to the wooden dock. The man with the striped shirt came back out. Flaco ducked behind a stack of wooden boxes on the dock.

Two other men came out of the cabin—the man with the beer bottle and another man. Both men were unshaven and dirty. All three men walked over to the gangplank.

"Flaco better watch out," Carlos whispered.

"We better move," Miguel warned as the men started down the gangplank.

Carlos and Miguel backed away from the truck. A few yards away was a rack holding a broken fish net. The two boys crouched down behind the netting. Carlos held his breath as the men came down the gangplank. None of the men noticed Flaco. As they got into the truck, Señor Revolver took the driver's seat.

"They're leaving," Miguel said.

"So is Flaco," Carlos said, pointing. Flaco walked rapidly down the dock and stood right behind the truck. The engine started. A puff of black smoke spewed out of the exhaust pipe. Flaco suddenly pulled himself up into the back of the truck just as it began to roll forward.

"He's getting into the truck!" Miguel said with alarm.

The truck gradually picked up speed as it rolled down the narrow road by the waterfront. Miguel and Carlos stood up from behind the nets. They could see Flaco climbing over the mounds of burlap sacks.

"What's he doing?" Miguel asked.

"I don't know, but let's see if we can find out." Carlos took off running after the truck. Miguel was right behind him.

Chapter Five

The Thief

Even running as hard as they could, Carlos and Miguel couldn't keep up with the truck. It turned the corner beyond the market street and disappeared going up the hill toward the plaza.

"I don't think we can catch it." Miguel was breathing hard.

"Me neither." Carlos slowed down. They turned on the street where the truck had turned, but the truck was out of sight.

"Let's go back to the plaza," Carlos said. "Maybe it stopped up there."

"Okay." Both boys walked quickly. Carlos was wondering the whole time why Flaco would climb into the back of the truck and what had happened to him.

When they got to the plaza, there were a few pickup trucks parked in front of Señora Garza's store, but not the big truck. Carlos had his hands on his hips as he surveyed the scene.

"I wish we could see that truck." Carlos scanned the plaza again.

"There's your mother and Julie," Miguel pointed out. Mrs. Brown and Julie were standing in front of the little police station. Deputy Sánchez and Señora Garza were talking with them. Mrs. Brown and Julie saw Carlos the same time he saw them. Mrs. Brown waved for Carlos to come over.

"Let's go see what she wants," Carlos said.

Even before they got closer, Carlos could tell it was bad news. Julie's nose was red and her eyes bleary. She looked as if she'd been crying.

"What happened?" Carlos asked. Señora Garza and Deputy Sánchez stepped back inside the police station.

"We have bad news," his mom said softly. "I can barely believe it. I can't believe it."

"Believe what?" Carlos asked.

"Pastor Pablo," Julie said.

"He didn't . . . he didn't die, did he?" Carlos asked. He felt a lump form in his throat.

"No, he didn't die," Mrs. Brown said. "But your father called. The reason that Pastor Pablo and the three children are so sick is because of drugs. Apparently they had some kind of drug overdose."

"¿Drogas?" Miguel asked in disbelief.

"Pastor Pablo takes drugs?" Carlos asked in amazement.

"I know it's hard to believe," his mom said. "They did blood tests on all four of them, and they found the same thing: high levels of cocaine."

"How could all this happen?" Carlos asked.

"I don't know." His mom got out a handkerchief to wipe her nose. "They're all still too sick to talk, which is why it's such a mystery. If we could only talk to them then we'd know what happened. Apparently the drugs were contaminated. Little Isabel is very sick, your father said. Pastor Pablo and the others aren't much better."

Carlos and Miguel didn't say anything for a few moments. No one spoke as the news sank in.

"Could they have made a mistake?" Carlos asked finally.

"The blood tests were conclusive," Mrs. Brown said. "I thought it was some kind of food poisoning. None of this makes any sense. We've known Pastor Pablo for years, and he's not the kind of man who uses drugs."

"I think somebody gave them drugs on purpose," Julie said. "Someone who doesn't like him."

"Yeah, I bet that's it," Carlos agreed. "Pastor Pablo wouldn't take drugs or give them to children."

"I can't believe that he would take drugs or that someone would hate him enough to do this," their mom said. "Who would want to hurt Pastor Pablo and innocent children?"

"Deputy Sánchez and Señora Garza know about the hospital's finding cocaine in their system, and soon the whole town will know," Julie said sadly. "They'll tell everybody."

"Does Deputy Sánchez think Pastor Pablo took drugs on purpose?" Carlos asked incredulously.

"He says they will have to investigate every angle," Julie replied. "But he says if Pastor Pablo took drugs on purpose that they would have to arrest him."

"Arrest him?" Carlos asked in surprise.

"He says he's heard rumors about Pastor Pablo that weren't good," his mom said. "I asked him to be more specific, but he just shrugged his shoulders. He acts like there may be something to the rumors."

"But you can't convict a person just because of rumors," Carlos protested.

"Rumors can ruin your reputation, even if you are innocent," his mom said. "If we don't get to the bottom of this soon, it may turn out very badly, even if Pastor Pablo did nothing wrong."

"Everyone gossips in a small town like Santiago," Julie said. "It will be a scandal. None of the churches will want to help out if Pastor Pablo gets arrested or if they hear about these rumors. Mom says the orphanage would shut down without Pastor Pablo."

"Shut down the orphanage?" Miguel asked. "But where will María and I go if they shut down the orphanage?"

"Where will all the other kids go?" Julie asked. "The whole thing is a terrible mess. Señora Garza said people are already talking about the orphanage's being haunted because of the ghost. Now things will just be worse."

"But they can't really believe in ghosts," Carlos said.

"It's a small town, and a lot of the people aren't very educated," Mrs. Brown said. "Señor Losada said his wife wants him to leave the orphanage because of the ghost story. Their cousins, the other staff members that help out, all refused to come in this morning. It's crazy, I know, but a lot of these people are convinced the orphanage is haunted. And once they hear that Pastor Pablo and the others overdosed on drugs, they may not care about what's really true. I'm afraid many people in town will want the orphanage to close down. It's a tragedy. Pastor Pablo led several people to Christ in the last few months in Santiago and other towns near here."

"There's more bad news for the orphanage besides that," Julie added.

"What's that?"

"Señora Garza said she saw someone shoplifting a package of expensive cassette tapes from her store this morning," Julie said. "She was complaining to Deputy Sánchez about it."

"Who was it?"

"She said she could only see his back," Julie replied. "He wore a blue Dallas Cowboys sweatshirt."

Carlos thought for a moment.

"Flaco has a shirt like that," Carlos said. "He was wearing it this morning."

"We know," their mom said. "Señora Garza and Deputy Sánchez want to come up to the orphanage to look around. We were just getting ready to go with them to search Flaco's room."

Just then, Señora Garza and Deputy Sánchez came back outside. Both looked very grim. Deputy Sánchez rode with Señora Garza in her black Cadillac. Mrs. Brown drove Carlos, Miguel and Julie up the road behind the Cadillac.

The orphanage was unusually quiet for a Saturday. Children wandered in groups around the playground, but very few were playing. The news had already spread about Pastor Pablo's being sick because of a drug overdose.

Mrs. Brown led Deputy Sánchez and Señora Garza inside. They walked to the dormitory rooms without speaking. When they reached Flaco's room, the door was open. Roberto lay on the bed reading a Mexican comic book. The big boy sat up when the others entered the room.

"We need to look around your room," Mrs. Brown said.

"Is there something wrong?" Roberto asked when he saw Deputy Sánchez.

"I hope not," Mrs. Brown said.

"Where does Flaco keep his things?" Deputy Sánchez asked.

"Those are his boxes by the bed over there." Roberto pointed to the bed. "The closet is mine. I was in this room first. He's only lived here six months."

Deputy Sánchez walked over and picked up three boxes and put them on the bed. He dumped out the first box. It was filled with pants and shirts. The second box was filled with socks and underwear. He dumped out the third box, which held a sweater, a jacket and a soccer ball.

"I don't see it," Deputy Sánchez said.

"See what?" Roberto asked with interest.

Deputy Sánchez picked up the jacket. He frowned. He unzipped the jacket. A small cassette player and a package of unopened cassette tapes fell out.

"¡Mis cintas!" Señora Garza pointed at the cassette tapes.

"That looks like Emily's cassette player too," Julie said.

"So he did steal it," Roberto said triumphantly. "I knew it. I thought he was acting suspicious. He denied everything, of course, because he is a liar as well as a thief."

"When did he steal the tapes?" Carlos asked.

"An hour ago exactly," Señora Garza said angrily as she looked at her watch.

"Do you know where Flaco is?" Deputy Sánchez asked Roberto.

"No, sir," Roberto replied. "I saw him walking toward town this morning, that's all I know. I was playing fútbol on the playground until a little while ago."

"We saw Flaco—"

Carlos hit Miguel in the ribs so hard that the little boy's glasses almost fell off his face. Miguel looked at Carlos with irritation and surprise.

"Where did you see Flaco?" the deputy asked.

"We saw him this morning at breakfast," Carlos said quickly. "And we saw him in town, but we don't know where he is now for sure."

"When you find Flaco, you need to call me or bring him to our office," Deputy Sánchez said to Mrs. Brown.

"I understand." Mrs. Brown's face looked more weary than Carlos had ever seen it.

The adults left the room talking about Flaco. Julie and Roberto followed them. Carlos motioned for Miguel to stay in the room. When the sound of the voices disappeared, Miguel spoke.

"Why did you hit me?" Miguel asked. "We know where Flaco is."

"Not really," Carlos replied. "We saw him get into that truck, but we don't know where the truck is, do we?"

"No. I guess not."

"I want to investigate further."

"But why?" Miguel asked. "They found the stolen cassette tapes and the tape player in Flaco's box."

"I still want to look around." Carlos began scanning the room. "Stand by the door and tell me if you see anyone coming."

"Okay." Miguel stood by the door as Carlos looked through the clothes spread out on Flaco's bed. Then he looked under his bed. Then he looked under Roberto's bed. "What are you doing?"

"Just looking around," Carlos said. He walked over to the closet and looked through the clothes hanging on the rod. He knelt down and looked inside the boxes on the floor of the closet. He picked up a pair of tennis shoes and examined them. He looked at the clothes in the closet again. A trash can was sitting in the corner of the room. It was filled with crumpled-up newspapers. Carlos dumped them out. The rest of the can was empty. Carlos began to uncrumple the newspapers.

"What are you doing?" Miguel demanded.

"Just looking around," Carlos said.

"At old newspapers?" Miguel asked. "You can't even read them because they're all dirty. You're making a mess."

"I just wanted to see if anything was inside the newspapers," Carlos replied.

"They're just trash and dirt," Miguel said.

"I know," Carlos said as bits of hard dirt fell onto the floor. He put the newspapers back into the trash can. Then he picked up the clumps of dirt with his fingers and put them in the trash can too.

"Let's get out of here," Miguel said. "If someone sees us looking around in here, they'll think we're thieves too, just like Flaco."

"You may be right," Carlos said with a smile.

"I bet the whole town thinks the orphanage is full of thieves," Miguel said. "Señora Garza will talk in her store and soon everyone will know. Flaco makes the rest of us look bad. Everyone in town will be talking about Pastor Pablo and the drugs. They'll shut down the orphanage, and María and I will be out on the street."

"That can't happen," Carlos said.

"Of course it can happen," Miguel said. "Your mother said they might close the orphanage. Didn't you hear her?"

"Yes," Carlos said softly.

"If it closes, we'll be on the street."

"You wouldn't just be dumped out with no place to live."

"Where would we go?" Miguel asked. Carlos didn't have an answer. "It could happen. Have you ever been to Mexico City? I have visited there. Lots of children live on the streets. Some live in cardboard boxes. Others live in the dumps. Antonio used to live on the street in Mexico City before he came here. He can tell you how hard it is. His grandmother brought him to Santa Anita before she died. He was lucky Pastor Pablo took him in, or else he might have ended up back on the street. When you leave, you get to go back to the United States to a good home. But what if they close the orphanage? Where will we all go, and who will take care of us?"

Carlos didn't say anything. The tears in Miguel's eyes couldn't hide the boy's fear. The small boy took off his broken glasses and wiped his eyes with his sleeve. "You don't know what it's like," Miguel said. "But I have my sister to protect. It's not easy for a girl. I could survive, I think, but it would be very hard for María. Do you know how dangerous it is for a little girl to live on the street? I would have to take care of her. Where will she go if the orphanage closes?"

"I don't know," Carlos said. He began to understand Miguel's fears as he put himself in Miguel's shoes. "But surely they won't close it. Somebody will do something, won't they?"

"You were blessed because you were adopted," Miguel said to Carlos. "If the Browns hadn't taken you in, where do you think you would be today? You could be living here. Or maybe you'd live in the street, or worse."

Carlos didn't say anything. He had lived with the Browns ever since he could remember. As far as he was concerned they were his mom and dad, and he was their son. For a moment he wondered what his life would have been like if he hadn't been adopted. He would probably be somewhere in Mexico, like Miguel said. Maybe he would have lived at the orphanage, or maybe it would have been worse. Carlos shuddered. He loved his family and knew they loved him. It was hard to imagine not being together as a family. His life seemed very safe and certain compared to Miguel's situation.

"God has to do something," Carlos said suddenly. "He can't let the orphanage close."

Carlos remembered the verses in the Bible about orphans and the fatherless. His father always read them to the church group before they left on their trips to Mexico.

"God especially loves the fatherless," Carlos said.

"Then why are there so many in the streets with no homes?" Miguel asked.

Carlos didn't have an answer. He thought of all the news reports he'd seen of poor countries where there were lots of orphans. Some were orphans because of wars, others because of poverty and sickness. Who knew all the reasons? It seemed too hard to understand.

"We have to keep praying," Carlos said defiantly. "And we have to keep investigating. I know something wrong is happening here, if I could just figure it out."

"What's wrong is Pastor Pablo's being on drugs," Miguel said in despair. "How could he do that? How could he do that to all of us?"

"I can't believe he did it," Carlos said, shaking his head. "He wouldn't give drugs to children either. That doesn't make any sense."

"But they are sick," Miguel replied.

"But he loves children," Carlos said. "His whole life was

taking care of kids here at the orphanage. It just doesn't add up."

"I thought that too," Miguel said. "He acted like he had so much fun with us at the birthday party. When the piñata broke, he was down on the ground helping the little children collect candy because they couldn't move as fast as the older kids. He helped Isabel gather candy because she wears a leg brace, remember?"

"He did help, didn't he?" Carlos said.

"Tell that to the people in town," Miguel said. "People do gossip and believe rumors. They will think this place is haunted, and now it's full of thieves and drug users. They'll be glad to see the orphanage shut down."

Carlos sat down on Flaco's bed. He didn't say a word. He looked down at his watch. He stared at the second hand slowly moving around the circle of numbers. Maybe time was running out for the orphanage. Maybe it would shut down. Carlos prayed that it wouldn't happen. He stared at his watch once more. Then his eyes opened wider.

"Maybe that's how it fits," Carlos said.

"How what fits?" Miguel asked.

"Let's get out of here."

"Where are we going?"

"Just help me out." Carlos ran out of the room. Miguel was close behind.

Chapter Six

Looking for Candy

Carlos ran into the main dining hall and then into the kitchen. He looked for his mother and Julie, but neither one was around. Señor Losada was arranging the tables for lunch. Since many of the adult helpers hadn't come in yet, the place seemed rather empty. The children were filing inside.

"Have you seen my mother?" Carlos had ideas about his investigation that he felt sure she would want to know.

"They left a little while ago," the older man said. His eyes looked sad. "There was some problem, and they went to town."

"But I have things I need to tell her," Carlos said.

"You'll have to wait until she returns." Señor Losada shrugged his shoulder and turned away to help the children eat. Carlos slapped his thigh in frustration.

"Mom needs to know about this stuff," Carlos said. "I wish

Dad were here."

"What stuff?" Miguel asked.

Carlos didn't say anything for a moment, lost in his own thoughts. Then his eyes brightened. "Do you know where Lucita lives?"

"Lucita?"

"The little girl at Isabel's birthday party," Carlos said. "After the party, Pastor Pablo took her home and then came back to the orphanage. Remember? Where does she live?"

"She lives south of town with her grandparents. Why?"

"We need to go there. We'll keep investigating until Mom and Dad get back."

"But why?"

"I want to check something out. Let's go." The two boys rushed out the front door and headed down the hill. They passed the old abandoned church and the place where the ghost had appeared. Miguel crossed to the other side of the street to be far away from the cemetery gate.

"This place still gives me the creeps," Miguel said.

"There's no reason to be afraid of any ghost," Carlos said confidently.

"Why not?"

"Because it doesn't exist," Carlos replied.

"But we saw it!"

"We saw someone pretending to be a ghost," Carlos said.

"Are you sure?" Miguel asked in surprise.

"I'm pretty sure," Carlos said. "But I'll explain it later. I have a theory."

"A what?"

"A theory; a kind of guess," Carlos said. "It's sort of like pieces of a puzzle, only the pieces aren't connected. Once you see enough pieces, you begin to guess what the puzzle looks like. Solving a mystery is like solving a puzzle."

"And you know what the puzzle looks like?"

"I think so. But I have to see a few more pieces before I can be sure. Let's hurry." Carlos began to jog slowly down the hill toward the plaza. Since it was around noon, several stores were closed for siesta or lunch. The plaza was mostly deserted. "Show me where Lucita lives."

"She lives this way," Miguel said, pointing.

Carlos followed Miguel. They passed the mercado street and kept going south. The southern part of Santiago was the poorer section of town. The streets were unpaved and full of drying mud. The houses were very small and made of brick or adobe. The yards had no grass—only dirt and mud. Very few had running water or bathrooms. Chickens and goats and turkeys roamed near some of the yards. Dogs barked as the two boys kept walking.

"Lucita lives at the end of the next street."

The two boys moved faster. When they got to the next street, they saw the police car at the end of the street. The red light was flashing around and around. A crowd of people were out in the tiny yard. "Looks like there's some sort of trouble," Miguel said.

The police car began moving down the dirt road away from the house. Sheriff Vega was driving. An old woman was in the back seat.

"Let's find out what happened," Carlos said. The two boys walked up to the crowd of people, who were talking in low voices. Some looked afraid. Others looked angry. Carlos couldn't understand them.

"What happened?" Carlos asked Miguel.

"They're talking about drugs and Pastor Pablo." Miguel listened some more. His face fell.

"What happened?"

"It's Lucita. She got sick and passed out. Just like Pastor Pablo and the other children. It looks like she took drugs too. They say they can't locate Deputy Sánchez. They said your mother and Julie took Lucita and her grandmother to the hospital."

"Mom and Julie went with them?" Carlos asked. "This must be the problem Señor Losada mentioned. This is horrible! I need to tell her what I think is going on." Carlos looked very perplexed.

"They will come back," Miguel said. He could see that his friend was upset.

"I know," Carlos said. "But we need to talk now. Is Lucita's grandfather here?"

"I don't see him," Miguel said. "He's a fisherman. He's probably out fishing."

"Let's look inside the house."

"I don't know if we should. These people are talking about the orphanage. Some are saying it's full of thieves and drug dealers. If they see us going into the house, we could get in trouble. They might think we're thieves."

"We need to get inside," Carlos insisted.

"We can try going in the back," Miguel said nervously. "But I don't think it's a good idea."

"We have to try," Carlos said firmly. Miguel looked unhappy as he led Carlos to the rear of the house. The two boys slipped through the crowd without attracting attention. All the neighbors were talking in small groups.

There was a door at the rear of the house made of roofing

tin nailed to a wooden frame. Carlos opened it carefully. He looked around to see if anyone was watching and then stepped inside the little shack of a house.

There were only three small rooms. The floor of the house was made of dusty bricks. The room he was in had two beds with old worn covers. One bed was full size and the other was smaller.

"That's probably Lucita's bed," Miguel said.

Carlos immediately began looking around the smaller bed. A wooden banana crate served as a little table and storage box. He looked through the box carefully. There was a worn dress and an old plastic doll missing one arm.

Carlos stood up. He was about to keep looking when he noticed a little girl standing in the doorway where they had entered.

"Hola," Carlos said awkwardly to the little girl. Miguel whirled around. He looked surprised and guilty. The little girl didn't say anything. She just stared at the two boys.

"Who is she?" Carlos asked.

"She's a cousin, I think." Miguel spoke to her in Spanish. The little girl answered in a tiny voice. "She is her cousin, and she wants to know what we're doing here."

"Ask her if she knows where Lucita keeps her candy."

"Her candy? Why would you want to know that?"

"Just ask her."

Miguel spoke to the little girl. She thought for a moment and then walked through the room into the next. A wooden table was surrounded by some wooden chairs. Behind that was a two-burner kerosene stove on a stand made of pipe. Above the stove were shelves. The little girl pointed up at the shelves filled with pots and pans and a few dishes.

"¡Allí!" the little girl said, pointing at a coffee can. Carlos reached up and got the coffee can. He looked inside and saw a little white paper sack with candy in it.

"That's from the party," Miguel said. "I have a sack like it."

"I know." Carlos opened the sack and emptied it out onto the table. There were lots of empty wrappers. There were five pieces of candy corn, two little boxes of sour balls and a red jawbreaker.

"What are you looking for?" Miguel asked. "It's just candy."

"I know." Carlos sounded disappointed. He looked at the pile of candy on the table. He picked up the pieces and dropped them back into the sack. The only things left were old candy wrappers. He grabbed the empty wrappers and started putting those into the sack. Then he stopped.

"I've got another idea," Carlos said. He spread the wrappers out on the table. He stared at them for a moment and then picked them up and stuffed them into his pocket. The little girl watched him suspiciously.

"I'm putting the candy back," Carlos said, dropping the little white sack into the coffee can. He put the can on the shelf.

"What are you doing?" Miguel asked.

"We need to get back to the orphanage." Carlos walked to the back of the house and out the back door. The little girl followed them to the street in front of the house. They made their way through the chattering crowd and then ran down the muddy street.

Carlos hurried up the hill toward the plaza. Going uphill was much more tiring than coming down. By the time they got to the orphanage, both boys were sweating. But Carlos was determined to keep investigating. The children had finished eating lunch and the long tables were folded up. Carlos looked for his mother and sister, but couldn't find them.

"Where did they go?" Carlos asked Señor Losada. The old man shrugged his shoulders.

"Let's go," Carlos whispered to Miguel. "We need to check Jorge, Ricardo and Isabel's rooms. They are the ones who got sick that night. Do you know which rooms they stay in?"

"Sure." Miguel led Carlos to the dormitory. They went to Ricardo's room first. No one was there. Carlos saw what he was looking for on the boy's bed. He reached up and grabbed a small white paper sack.

"That's Ricardo's candy sack," Miguel said. Carlos took out a pen and wrote Ricardo's name on the sack.

"Let's go to Jorge's room." Carlos took the sack with him.

"Won't you get in trouble for stealing the candy?" Miguel asked.

"I'll return everything," Carlos replied as they walked down the hall. They went into Jorge's room next.

"See if you can find his candy sack," Carlos said. Both boys searched in all of Jorge's things, but they didn't find it.

"Maybe he ate it all," Miguel said.

"Maybe. But where would you hide your candy if you had it?"

Miguel looked slowly around the room. Then he climbed up on Jorge's bunk and lifted up his pillow. A little white paper sack was lying halfway under the sheet.

"Good job." Carlos took out his pen and wrote Jorge's name on the bag. The boys then walked over to the girls' side of the dormitory.

"Hello?" shouted Carlos. "Anyone over here?"

Carmen popped her head out of the first door.

"Where's Isabel's room?"

"She stays in this room," Carmen said.

"Can we come in?" Carlos asked.

Carmen opened the door wider and waved them in.

"Did she bring back any candy from the birthday party?" Carlos asked.

"I think so." Carmen lifted a box from under the bed. She showed them a new doll and a new skirt. "She got these at the party, and here is her candy." She pulled out a white paper sack.

"We need to borrow it," Carlos said. "We promise we won't take any candy."

Carlos wrote Isabel's name on the sack. He looked around the room. His eyes lit up when he saw a bright paper head of a parrot sitting on a bookshelf by the bed.

"The head of the piñata." Carlos picked it up.

"She thought it was too pretty to throw away," Carmen said. "She wanted to keep it."

"It is pretty." Carlos turned to Miguel. "We need to keep moving."

Carlos left the room carrying the three sacks of candy. Miguel followed him outside to a small house behind the dining hall. Carlos opened the door of the house.

"We aren't supposed to go in Pastor Pablo's house without permission," Miguel said slowly.

"It's an emergency. Trust me." Carlos went inside. Miguel looked around to see if anyone was watching. Then he followed Carlos inside. He kept looking behind him. The front room of the house was Pastor Pablo's study. A big desk was on the right side of the room. On top of the desk was a small white sack. Carlos picked it up. He frowned when he found the sack empty. He looked all around the desk. He smiled when he found the trash can. He picked it up and dumped it out on the floor. He studied the contents: a dried, blackened banana peel, an old magazine, a broken pencil and a piece of blue cellophane. Carlos picked up the blue cellophane.

"What's that?" Miguel asked.

"I'm not sure. Empty out each bag of candy onto the floor. See if any of the candy has a wrapper with this kind of blue cellophane."

Miguel did as he was told. All the candy looked like familiar brands. Some was unwrapped candy corn. None of the candy was wrapped with blue cellophane.

Then Carlos pulled out the used candy wrappers he had gotten from Lucita's house. "There." He picked up one of the wrappers. It was a light blue square of cellophane, just like the one found in Pastor Pablo's trash can.

"It's just a candy wrapper," Miguel said.

"But for what kind of candy?"

"I don't know." Miguel said after a moment. "What difference does it make?"

"You mean you don't recognize the wrapper?" Carlos asked excitedly.

"No."

"Neither do I," Carlos replied. "That's the point. This might not have been candy at all but something else."

"What do you mean, 'something else'? If it wasn't candy, then what else could it be?"

"Drugs. The drugs that made Pastor Pablo and Jorge, Ricardo, Isabel and Lucita all sick."

"But why would it just be them?" Miguel asked. "That doesn't make sense. Why haven't any others gotten sick?"

"Remember the night of the party?" Carlos asked. "Pastor Pablo drove Lucita to her home. Ricardo, Jorge and Isabel were in the car with him. All those children got sick."

"That's why the police think Pastor Pablo gave them drugs—because he was alone with them in the car," Miguel said. "Now with Lucita getting sick, it looks even worse for Pastor Pablo because she was in the car too. Maybe he gave her some drugs, but she didn't take them till today."

"That could be true," Carlos said. "But I don't believe Pastor Pablo would take drugs or give drugs to anyone else. I think there's another explanation."

"What?"

"I think they ate drugs that looked like candy," Carlos said. "Don't you see? That *would* make sense. They wouldn't know they were taking drugs. It could be drugs that looked or tasted like candy."

"I don't know," Miguel said doubtfully. "I never heard of drugs looking like candy."

"It's possible," Carlos said. "People do all sorts of clever things to disguise drugs. You see it on the television news all the time."

"But why would just those five get sick?" Miguel asked. "We all had candy from the piñata. No one else is sick."

"I know," Carlos said with a frown. "That's the only part that doesn't fit yet, but the rest of the pieces . . ." Carlos stopped. "Wait a minute. Maybe there is an answer. Let's go."

Carlos jumped and headed for the door, leaving the candy and paper bags strewn all over the floor of Pastor Pablo's office. He hit the door running. Miguel sped after him.

Carlos ran across the yard to the dormitory. He dashed down the hallway and stopped at Isabel's room. Carmen was sitting at her desk reading a Bible.

"Carmen, I need to borrow this too." Carlos pointed to the bright parrot head sitting on the shelf. Carlos picked up the head of the piñata. He was coming out the door as Miguel ran up.

"Let's go back to the office." Carlos carried the head upside down.

"What are you doing?"

"You'll see," Carlos said. When they got back inside Pastor Pablo's office, Carlos closed the door carefully and locked it.

Carlos examined the head of the parrot closely. He reached inside the hollow head and felt inside for over a minute. He looked disappointed when all he brought out were strips of paper. He picked up the head and shook it. He heard a rattling sound.

"Something's inside there," Miguel said. Carlos tipped the head and shook it again, holding it up to his ear. He listened to the rattle. He shook the head harder. "It's up in the beak of the parrot."

Carlos tipped the piñata head and shook it again. The rattling stopped as something fell out of the bird head. On the floor in front of them were three pieces of candy wrapped in blue cellophane. Carlos unwrapped one. Inside was a white round ball a little smaller than a jawbreaker. The candies looked like moth balls to Carlos. The wrapper was identical to the one he found in Pastor Pablo's trash can and the one in Lucita's bag of candy.

"Have you ever seen candy like this before?" Carlos asked in a whisper.

"Never. Do you think it's—"

"Drugs. I'm almost sure of it. We can take it to the police and they can test it."

"Drogas . . ." Miguel stared at the white balls.

Suddenly there was a banging on the door. Carlos jumped.

"Open the door! Open the door!" a voice yelled. The banging grew louder.

Chapter Seven

Looking for a Ghost

Miguel stood up and peeked out the window. He looked relieved.

"It's only Roberto," he said.

"I'm not surprised," Carlos said. "But we can't let him know what we found out or what we were doing."

"Why not?" Miguel said. "If those pieces of candy are really drugs, this proves that Pastor Pablo and the others took the drugs by mistake."

"I know," Carlos said. "But we can't mention this to anyone. There's still more work to be done. Just don't tell Roberto anything we found out. I have a plan. Just follow along with me."

"Open the door!" Roberto shouted from the outside.

Carlos scooped up the candy and wrappers off the floor and put them back in the bags. He took the three blue-wrapped candy balls and put them in his pocket. He put the parrot head under his arm. Roberto was still banging when Carlos unlocked and opened the door. He was hitting the door so hard that Carlos had to duck to miss being hit by the other boy. "Almost got my nose," Carlos said with a laugh.

"What are you two doing in here?" Roberto suspiciously looked all around the room and then back at Carlos. "No one is allowed in here unless they have permission."

"I know," Carlos said. "How did you know we were here?"

"I saw you come in," Roberto asked. "So I came over to see what you were doing."

"We've been investigating a few things," Carlos said.

"You have? Like what?"

"I was hoping we might find the ghost everyone is so scared of," Carlos said.

"You think the ghost lives in Pastor Pablo's house? You're loco."

"We didn't find the ghost in here, did we?" Carlos said to Miguel.

"That's right," Miguel said slowly. "We didn't find any ghost in here."

"Of course you didn't," Roberto said. "The ghost lives at the graveyard, they say. But why do you have the head of that piñata?"

"This head?" Carlos held it out. "I thought there might be a clue inside it."

"A clue for the ghost?" Roberto asked.

"Maybe," Carlos said. "It could be clues for other things."

"What other things?" Roberto asked with great interest. "What do you know that you aren't telling?"

"I can't say until we know for sure," Carlos said.

"Are you talking about the drugs?" Roberto asked.

"Who said anything about drugs?" Carlos asked. "We were talking about the ghost."

"But you said . . ." Roberto grew quiet as he stared at the papier-mâché head. Carlos placed the head of the parrot on Pastor Pablo's desk. Then he walked to the door.

"What are you doing?" Roberto asked.

"I think we need to leave it locked up here," Carlos said. "The police can examine it later."

"The police?" Roberto asked.

"We better get out of here now." Carlos motioned for the two boys to go outside. Carlos carefully pushed the button on the doorknob to lock it and then pulled the door tight.

Once outside, he began walking across the yard toward the big meeting hall. Roberto and Miguel ran after him.

"I think I know where the ghost lives," Carlos said. "And I think Flaco knows too."

"Flaco!" Roberto said. "He's a thief and a liar. Whatever he tells you is a lie."

"Maybe." Carlos rounded the corner. He kept walking until he got to the window.

"What did Flaco say about the ghost?" Roberto asked.

"He said that the ghost may have turned out the lights last night," Carlos replied coolly.

"How could Flaco know such a thing?" Roberto spat on the ground.

"That's what I wondered," Carlos replied. "But then I got to thinking about it. I wondered how a ghost could turn out the lights. But it wouldn't be so hard. The ghost was standing outside this window. And the breaker box is fifteen feet away."

Carlos pointed to the breaker box at the corner of the building. He walked over to it. He flipped up the metal lid.

"All our ghost would have to do is flip that big switch and the lights would go right out," Carlos said.

"But a ghost can't move things," Roberto said. "They can't turn switches on and off."

"Probably not," Carlos agreed. "But I could turn it off. Or Flaco. Or Miguel or even you. You could just flip that big breaker and the lights would go right out, wouldn't they?"

"But the storm turned off the lights," Roberto insisted. "That's what all the others believe."

"But I believe in facts," Carlos said. "The lights in town were still on last night. I'm convinced that our ghost turned off this switch."

"Really?" Roberto said.

"But, you see, I don't think it was a ghost at all," Carlos said. "I think it was someone pretending to be a ghost. And I think his fingerprints will be on the switch still. There would be Señor Losada's fingerprints because he turned it back on. And there would be the fingerprints of our ghost."

"Fingerprints?" Roberto asked. "Would a ghost have fingerprints?"

"A ghost wouldn't, but a person like you or me would," Carlos said. He closed the lid of the circuit-breaker box tightly. "In fact, I'm going to have Sheriff Vega or Deputy Sánchez try to get fingerprints off the switch to see if I'm right."

"But how could someone pretend to be a ghost?" Roberto asked in disbelief. "We all saw it. It looked so real. It didn't look like a person to me."

"Well, I've been thinking hard about that all day," Carlos said. "I didn't really have an answer until I looked at my watch this afternoon while we were in your room. You know, after they found the stolen cassette player and tapes."

"Go on," the large boy said curiously.

"We have to go inside for me to show you." Carlos led the others inside the dining hall. Near the door was a closet. He opened the door, and the other boys followed him inside. The closet held brooms and a big industrial sink. Once they were inside, Carlos closed the door.

"What are you doing?" Miguel asked. "It's too dark in here."

"Are you trying to scare us?" Roberto asked.

"Not at all," Carlos replied. "Look at my wristwatch. What time is it, Roberto?"

"How would I know?"

"Look at my watch. Can't you see the time?"

Roberto looked down. In the dark he saw the glowing green dots on the hands and numbers of the wristwatch.

"It glows in the dark," Miguel said.

"Yes, it does," Carlos replied. "And it's two-thirty. Look at it, and you can see it."

"You're right," Miguel said. "That's a nice watch."

"Can you see it, Roberto?" Carlos asked.

"Yes, . . . but now I can't see it. What happened? No, there it is. It's two-thirty, like you said."

"Watch it closely," Carlos instructed the others in the dark. "Now, like a magician, I will make it disappear. Whoosh!"

"Hey, where did it go?" Miguel asked.

"I can't see it either," Roberto said.

Carlos opened the door slowly. As the boys got used to the light, they could see that Carlos was covering the watch with his right hand.

"No wonder we couldn't see it," Miguel said. "You were covering it with your hand."

"And that's the way our ghost appeared and disappeared," Carlos announced proudly.

"What do you mean?" Miguel asked.

"I knew it by the color," Carlos said. "I couldn't figure out why something about the ghost seemed familiar. But that shade of green is common in paint that glows in the dark. All our ghost had to do was have a black costume shaped like a ghost and covered with luminous paint. If it was very dark, like last night, you could cover up the costume with something dark, then uncover it. You could make the ghost appear and disappear instantly like it did at the window last night, and earlier at the graveyard."

"You could do it that way, couldn't you?" Miguel looked at his friend with new admiration.

"That's crazy," Roberto said. "I don't think it would work. Besides, why would someone do that?"

"Maybe so people would think that the orphanage was haunted," Carlos said.

"For what reason?" Roberto asked.

"I'm not sure yet, but I'm getting closer to an explanation," Carlos said with confidence. "In fact, I have some ideas. I'm going to tell the police and let them investigate. But first I have to find the ghost costume. And I think I know where it is."

"How would you know that?" Roberto asked.

"I think Flaco tipped me off," Carlos said.

"Flaco?" Roberto asked. "You mean you think he is pretending to be the ghost?"

"I'm not sure," Carlos said. "But I'll know when I find the costume. I'm going to look for it next. Do you want to come with us?"

"Uh, I don't know," Roberto said. "Where are you going

to look?"

"Like I said, I think Flaco may have given me the hint I was looking for. I think it may be hidden in the old church. Or it may be right here in the orphanage. But I think the church would make the best hiding place, don't you?"

"I don't know," the big boy said slowly. "I think the whole thing is a waste of time. Go look in the church. Just be careful because it's dangerous in there."

"We'll see you later." Carlos grabbed Miguel by the arm and walked outside.

"What are you doing?" Miguel asked.

"Trying to catch our ghost," Carlos said.

"Down at the old church?"

"No, I think we'll find him right here, but we better be quick," Carlos said. "Follow me."

Carlos crouched down and ran around to the side of the meeting hall. He looked inside just in time to see Roberto walk into the kitchen.

"Let's go." Carlos, still crouching down, ran all the way around to the kitchen window, started to stand up and peeked in. Miguel was beside him.

"I don't see anything," Miguel said. "The kitchen is empty."

"Wait. Watch the pantry door."

Almost as soon as he said it, the pantry door opened up. Miguel gasped when he saw Roberto come out of the pantry holding a big brown bag.

"Roberto is in the pantry," Miguel whispered. "But what's he got in the sack?"

"I think it's the ghost costume."

"He's the ghost?"

"I think so."

"But how did you guess it was him?" Miguel asked.

"I'll have to explain later," Carlos replied. "Now we need to watch what he does and where he goes."

Roberto grabbed a rag off the kitchen sink and went back into the big meeting hall.

"Hurry!" Carlos said. "We have to be careful he doesn't see us."

He crouched down and ran around to the far side of the meeting hall. Miguel was right behind. When he got to the corner, he peeked around it. At the far end of the building, Roberto was standing by the breaker box, rubbing the main breaker handle with the rag.

"He's wiping off his fingerprints," Carlos said. "I must have really scared him."

"We must catch him," Miguel said angrily. "He is the ghost! He scared everyone!"

"Not yet," Carlos replied.

"Why not?"

"Because we need the little ghost to lead us to the big ghost," Carlos said.

"The big ghost? Who's the big ghost?"

"That's what I want to find out. I think I know, but I'm not sure yet. Or why."

Roberto closed the lid to the breaker box. He looked around nervously. He tucked the paper bag under his arm and headed down the driveway.

"Let's go," Carlos said. They ran to the corner of the building. Roberto was already at the end of the driveway. The large boy ran awkwardly down the cobblestone street toward town. Carlos smiled at Miguel. The boys took off after the ghost.

Chapter Eight

The Mountain Road

Even though he was a slow runner, keeping up with Roberto wasn't easy. Carlos and Miguel had to stay far enough behind him so he wouldn't know he was being followed. Yet they had to be close enough to see where he went. Carlos stayed to the side of the curving road as much as possible.

Once in town, Roberto ran straight into the plaza. He disappeared behind the corner of the big church.

"Hurry or we'll lose him," Carlos said. He ran as fast as he could. Miguel had a hard time keeping up. Carlos reached the corner of the building first. He stopped and watched. Miguel came up behind.

"Just what I thought," Carlos said.

"He's going into Señora Garza's store," Miguel said. "Why would he do that?"

"Maybe she's the big ghost," Carlos said.

"Really?"

"I think so."

"How do you know?"

"I can't tell you now," Carlos said. "We need to get over there as fast as we can without being seen. If we go straight across the plaza, we'll be right out in the open."

"We can go around the plaza and come up to the rear of the store," Miguel said.

"Let's do it fast," Carlos replied. Miguel nodded and began running. They ran behind the church, then crossed the corner and ran behind the row of buildings to the east of the plaza, behind Señor Gómez's store. They cut across the mercado street into the alley. They ran down the alley and peeked around the corner.

"There's Señora Garza's store," Miguel said.

"And look what's behind it," Carlos added. "It's that truck we saw down at the dock by the boat."

The large truck was backed up to a large metal garage door at the rear of the store. Carlos studied the truck. He didn't see any of the men from the boat. He wondered if Flaco could still be in the back.

"We need to get closer," Carlos said. Miguel nodded in agreement.

Carlos ran across the street to the side of Señora Garza's store. Miguel followed as closely as a shadow. He walked to the corner that looked out over the plaza. He turned the corner and stepped quietly to the window on the front of the store. Cautiously he stuck his face up to the glass.

"What do you see?" Miguel whispered.

"Roberto is by the counter talking to Señora Garza," Carlos said. "He still has the package under his arm. Those three guys from the boat are inside drinking beer; nobody else is there. Señora Garza doesn't look very happy."

"I wish we could hear what they're saying," Miguel said.

"Wait a minute," Carlos said. "Everyone is getting up. Señora Garza and Roberto just went through the door leading to the back of the store. The three men are following her."

"Let's go look around back," Miguel said.

The two boys ran back across the street to the alley where they had been before. They crouched down behind a barrel and waited. The big metal garage door rolled up. The three men from the boat came outside and got into the truck. A few seconds later it started up and moved down the alley. Señora Garza's big black Cadillac rolled out of the garage. Roberto was in the front seat next to the big woman.

The Cadillac came straight down the alley toward Carlos and Miguel. Both boys slid behind the barrel as far as they could go. Fortunately, the Cadillac turned at the corner and headed into the plaza. The big truck followed the black car.

"We have to follow it," Carlos yelled. Both boys ran across the street to the corner of the plaza. The Cadillac and the truck turned at the corner on the north side of the plaza and headed up a road.

"That's the mountain road," Miguel said.

"Where does it go?"

"Into the mountains."

"I figured that," Carlos said. "But I meant to what towns?"

"All kinds of little towns and villages are in the mountains," Miguel replied. "They say if you follow the road far enough it goes all the way to Mexico City."

"We need to follow them," Carlos said impatiently. "I wish my mom and dad were here. I need to tell them what we've discovered. Maybe we could tell the police."

"They are not there," the smaller boy said, pointing at the station. "If there is no police car in front of their office, that means they are gone."

"We have to tell somebody," Carlos said frantically.

"The truck will soon be gone," Miguel said, looking sadly across the plaza.

"But how can we follow them?"

"Do you have money?" Miguel said.

"Some," Carlos replied. "I've got five dollars."

"We could use a taxi then," Miguel said. "Rolando's taxi is right over there in front of Señor Gómez's store."

"I don't know," Carlos said doubtfully.

"He's a good man," the smaller boy said. "He's been to church with us many times. If we don't go now, we may never find out where the truck goes."

"I know," Carlos said anxiously. "And Roberto has the costume with him."

"Maybe we can find where it goes and then have Rolando bring us back," the smaller boy said. "Then we can tell your parents."

"That sounds safe enough," Carlos said. "I hope my parents won't get mad. We better hurry."

The two boys ran across the plaza to the ancient black-and-white taxi. An older man sat snoozing in the front seat. A baseball cap was pulled down over his eyes. Miguel banged on the door and began talking. Carlos didn't catch a word he said. At first the old man shook his head as if refusing to go. Finally he seemed to reconsider.

"Show him your money," Miguel said. Carlos quickly got the money out of his wallet. He waved the dollar bills in front of the old man's face. The old man smiled. Miguel opened the back door of the cab. "Get in."

"Did you bargain with him?" Carlos asked.

"I didn't have time," Miguel said as he shut the door. The engine turned over and over and over. Carlos was beginning to think they'd made a mistake.

"¡Rápido!" Carlos said to the driver. "You should have bargained with him, Miguel."

"Relax," Miguel said. "Just make sure you don't give him the money until we get where we are going."

The old man got out of the cab and opened the hood of the car. He fiddled with something under the hood and then got back in the driver's seat. He tried the engine again, and it finally started. Then he got back out of the car and closed the hood.

"They'll be halfway to Mexico City by the time we get out of Santiago," Carlos grumbled. "This car must be forty years old."

"Maybe," Miguel said. "But Rolando loves this car."

"You should have bargained with him." Carlos didn't like the idea of losing all five dollars. He had worked hard for the money. Yet at the same time, if it helped solve a crime, it was well worth it.

The old man smiled as he got back into the car. He was missing half of his front teeth. He put the taxi in gear, and it headed out across the plaza.

They turned onto the narrow mountain road and started going up the first foothill. They passed several small streets with nicer homes off to the sides of the mountain road. Carlos and Miguel looked down each one trying to see the truck or car.

As they started down the hill, the cobblestones ended and the road was covered with gravel. They passed the last house in Santiago and entered the countryside. Green tropical plants and trees covered the first valley. They splashed through a creek that ran across the road and started uphill.

"I hope we can catch up," Carlos said impatiently. "Can't you get him to go faster?"

Miguel leaned over the front seat to talk. The old man shook his head, protesting.

"He's says were going as fast as we can uphill," Miguel said.

Carlos leaned forward to look over the edge of the seat. The speedometer registered zero. The big long needle jumped up every once in a while, but mostly it stayed down.

"His speedometer doesn't work," Carlos said with disgust.

"I hope the brakes work."

"Quit kidding."

"I'm not kidding," Miguel said. "Two weeks ago he ran right up onto the steps of the church in the plaza because his brakes went out. That's what everyone says. He almost ran over Señor Gómez's wife. The people in town said the car wanted to go to church. They thought it was funny."

"That doesn't sound too funny to me," Carlos said. A dull thumping noise came from below his feet. He cocked his head, listening carefully, wondering what was causing the noise. He couldn't come up with an answer. He sat back uneasily. The taxi picked up speed as it went downhill. The countryside flew by. The thumping noise beat faster as the car sped up. Carlos began praying silently.

"Maybe you should get him to test the brakes," Carlos

suggested nervously.

"Don't worry about it. Rolando knows what he's doing." Carlos relaxed. "I hope," Miguel added, and Carlos prayed twice as hard.

"I can't see anything with all this jungle around us," Carlos complained. The tall green trees had broad leaves.

"The river is off to our right," Miguel said. Through the tall trees Carlos saw occasional glimpses of greenish water. The taxi hit a bump in the road and rattled and bounced. Carlos bounced up so hard that he hit his head on the ceiling.

"Can't he watch what he's doing?" Carlos asked.

"You told him to go fast," Miguel replied.

"This taxi seems as if it would fall apart if it went over thirty miles an hour," Carlos replied. He began praying again as he looked around the inside of the old cab. A plastic saint was glued to the dashboard, a cross on a silver chain dangled from the rear-view mirror, and a black-and-white photograph of a woman was attached to the visor. Across the top of the windshield hung a string of green and red pom-poms. It reminded Carlos of decorations on a Christmas tree.

The car slowed down as it went up another winding hill. As it started down the other side, the old taxi sped around the curves on the narrow winding road. Carlos peered out the windshield, hoping to catch a glimpse of the truck or Cadillac. The longer they drove, the more remote the countryside became. They passed several men with burros and sheep along the road.

Once they had to pull way over to the edge of a cliff to let a small bus pass. It was so close that Carlos could have reached out the window and touched it. After the bus passed, the cab headed down the mountain. Carlos could see a tiny village down below. He whistled when he saw a truck at the outskirts of the village.

"That's it," Carlos said, pointing. Miguel nodded.

"I hope the truck stops soon," Miguel said. "I don't know if Rolando will go much farther for the money we agreed to pay him. We have to get back to town too."

Carlos shook his head and began praying again. The old cab drove into town.

"Santa Anita," Rolando said.

"That's the name of this town," Miguel said.

The town was two rows of small houses and shacks along both sides of the road. At the far end of the town were a few bodegas. A smaller road turned off the main one that ran through town.

"I think we saw the truck on that road, don't you?" Carlos asked.

"Maybe," Miguel said. "We can ask."

Miguel told Rolando to slow down. An old woman weaving a basket sat in front of a house next to the street. Miguel leaned out the window to talk to the woman.

"This is it," Miguel said with relief. "She says this road goes to a little warehouse owned by Señora Garza. It's just over the hill a few hundred yards away. Some of the people in town work for her. What should we do now?"

"I think we should go on foot and have Rolando wait here," Carlos said. "Maybe we can sneak up and find out what's going on. Then we can get back to town fast and hope my mom and dad are back."

Miguel spoke to Rolando, and the old man turned off the engine.

"He wants three dollars now," Miguel said.

"But we have to go back to Santiago still," Carlos protested.

"He said he'll wait thirty minutes," Miguel said. "But he still wants three dollars now. We can give him the other two dollars when we get back to Santiago."

"Oh, all right," Carlos said reluctantly, digging in his pocket. He pulled out three dollar bills. The old man smiled as he took the money.

"He says he'll wait only thirty minutes," Miguel warned. "So we better hurry. I think he'll wait."

"He better wait," Carlos said angrily. "Tell him to wait for us. We paid him."

"He already has your money," Miguel replied. "It might have been a mistake to give it to him first."

"You said he wanted it," Carlos moaned. "I did what you told me to do."

"I know, but maybe we could have made him wait," Miguel said. "It's too late now."

"You should have bargained more in the first place," Carlos said in exasperation. "Let's go."

The boys ran up the narrow muddy road. They ran inside the deep tire tracks left by the truck because the ground was firmer there. When they reached the top of the hill, they slowed down to a walk. They kept going until they could see the top of the truck. Then they hid behind a tree to watch.

Down below, the truck was parked next to a long, low building with a flat tin roof. There were only a few small windows. The Cadillac was parked next to the truck. Four bicycles and a motorcycle were nearby under a tree. Several men were busy unloading the big burlap sacks from the truck and carrying them into the building.

"If we go around to that side, the men in the truck won't see us," Carlos said. "We can find out what they're up to and then get back to Rolando and go tell my mom and dad."

"Okay," Miguel whispered. "Just watch out for snakes."

"Snakes?" Carlos asked in alarm.

Miguel nodded seriously. "There are lots of snakes around here. Some are very poisonous. It would be bad to get bitten."

Carlos began praying again. The two boys walked back behind the hill and began to circle around through the heavy tropical undergrowth. Every vine and bent tree branch suddenly looked like a snake to Carlos. After a few steps, he let Miguel lead the way. Carlos knew there were deadly snakes in Mexico. The only problem was that he wasn't sure what any of them looked like.

They moved slowly through the dense brush. Miguel then moved back over the hill. From that angle, they could go down to the shack without being seen by the men unloading the truck. The tin building had no windows on that side.

They picked their way downhill through plants and trees. Carlos kept trying to watch the building and where he was stepping at the same time. Several times he stepped on the back of Miguel's heels.

"Watch it!" Miguel snapped.

"Sorry," Carlos said.

After a few more nerve-wracking moments in the dense brush, they reached the clearing by the building. They ran to the rear of the building and edged along the tin siding. They peeked around the corner and saw a window just a few feet away.

Carlos ran to the window and tried to see through it, but it was too dirty. He rubbed it with his forearm. When the dirt came off, he could finally see inside. He jerked his head back quickly.

"Run!" he whispered. He pushed Miguel back toward the corner of the building. They had just rounded the corner when the window pushed open from the inside. Señora Garza stuck her head out the window and looked both ways.

Around the corner of the building, Carlos was holding on to Miguel so the boy wouldn't run into the brush. He was sure the big woman would see if they made a run for it. But maybe she had already seen them, he thought. He held his breath. Both boys waited silently, frozen in their place.

Chapter Nine

Inside the
Warehouse

Carlos and Miguel stayed pressed against the building for what seemed like an eternity, but no one came after them. Finally, Carlos pulled Miguel toward the other side of the building. The two boys walked as quietly as they could down to the opposite corner. Carlos cautiously stuck his head around the corner. As he did, he noticed a large rusty tear in the tin siding. By looking through the hole, they wouldn't have to risk going around the corner.

Both boys peered inside. At the far end of the building the men were still unloading the big burlap bags. Further inside, two men were opening the burlap sacks by pulling a thick piece of string. When the sack was opened, they tipped it into a large round tub. Raw green coffee beans spilled out into the tub like a river. Señora Garza and the man from the boat with the pistol stood next to the men pouring out the coffee beans.

Suddenly three white plastic packages fell out of the sack. Señor Revolver grabbed two of the bags and Señora Garza grabbed the other one.

"Drogas," Miguel whispered. Carlos nodded.

The man with the gun slit open the bag with a long switchblade knife. He opened it up and poured it out on a table.

"Dulces," the man said and laughed.

" 'Candy,' " Miguel translated.

"I know that word," Carlos whispered. Hundreds of pieces of the "candy" fell onto the table as the man emptied the bag. They were all wrapped with blue cellophane wrappers. They looked exactly like the three pieces Carlos had in his pocket. Señora Garza snapped her fingers. Two small old women quickly came over and scraped the candy-shaped drugs into a basket. They carried the basket over to another table. A piñata of a large colorful parrot lay on the table. One woman popped off the bird's head. They both began stuffing the candy-shaped drugs into the big paper bird's head. Then they stuffed the head with newspaper to keep the candy in place. They set the head to one side and began putting the drugs wrapped in blue into the bird's body. When all the drugs were gone, they stuffed newspapers into the rest of the body. One of the women then stuck the parrot's head back on the body with tape. Señora Garza smiled with satisfaction as they worked.

"That's how the drugs got in the bird's head," Carlos whispered.

"But why wasn't the rest of the piñata filled with drugs?"

Miguel asked.

"I don't know." Then Carlos's eyes opened wide. "They must have made some kind of mistake. I bet that's it. That's why!"

"Ssshhhhhh!" his small friend warned.

"Don't you see?" Carlos lowered his voice to a whisper. "I bet they put a drug-filled head on a regular empty body. Isabel kept the head because she thought it looked pretty. I bet she discovered there was more candy inside the head when they were in the car with Pastor Pablo. She must have given everyone some of the drugs, thinking it was more candy. That's why only those five got sick."

"You may be right," Miguel said.

"It has to be right or everyone else would have gotten sick from drugs too. Wait till my mom and dad and the sheriff hear about this."

"We better go now."

"Wait." Carlos wanted a better look around.

He stared inside the building. Off to one side were hundreds of the colorful piñatas shaped like birds, big lizards and turtles. Next to the piñatas were several open crates and boxes of firecrackers and fireworks.

"¡Rápido!" Señora Garza shouted at the two women. Their hands began moving faster. While men put the coffee beans back into the sack, two other men poured out another burlap bag of coffee beans. About halfway through the sack, three white plastic bags fell into view. More drug candies fell into view as other bags were cut open.

"She must sell these at the border or take them across into the United States," Carlos said.

"It must be worth a lot of money," Miguel added. "We

better go back now."

Señora Garza watched the operation carefully. She reached into her purse and pulled out a cellular phone. She dialed a few numbers and waited. She talked softly for a moment. As she talked, she began to scowl. She hung up the phone and dialed another number. She talked rapidly and then closed the phone. She looked around the room carefully.

"¡Roberto!" she yelled.

The large boy, munching on a long candy bar, appeared at the far end of the building. Señora Garza took him to one side and whispered to him. Roberto nodded and ran back outside.

"What's going on?" Carlos whispered.

"I don't know," Miguel replied. "I think we should go now."

"You're right," Carlos said. "I've seen all—"

"¡Señora! ¡Señora!" a voice shouted behind them. Carlos and Miguel jerked around. Roberto was looking right at them. Behind him was one of the men from the boat.

"Run!" Carlos yelled. Miguel didn't have to be told twice. The two boys turned the corner. They ran down along the long side of the building. Carlos was hoping they could turn the corner and get beyond the truck and Cadillac. But as they approached the corner, the man with the gun and Señora Garza rushed outside, cutting off their escape.

"Grab them!" the big woman yelled.

Carlos veered to the left and headed into the thick under-growth of the jungle. Miguel was right behind. They jumped over several fallen trees and slid down a steep bank.

"We need to head back toward town," Carlos yelled to his friend.

"Which way is town?" Miguel asked.

"I think it's that way." Carlos pointed quickly. He ducked

under a large branch and headed deeper into the forest. Behind them they could hear voices shouting that sounded close. Carlos tried running faster, but the thick limbs and branches tore at his legs and arms.

He jumped across a small ravine and tried to go uphill. But as he got higher, he reached a rocky cliff. The voices shouted above them. Carlos was about to run back down the small hill when he saw a hole in the rocks. He motioned for Miguel to follow him.

He pulled himself over a boulder toward the hole. The space wasn't really a cave, but it was big enough to crouch down inside. A ledge of rock acted as a roof. All around were other tall rocks. A person would have to be looking right down into the hole to see the two boys.

Carlos scrunched down as far as possible and made room for Miguel. Both boys were breathing hard. The air was thick and humid in the tropical foliage. Sweat rolled down Carlos's cheek.

The pursuing voices grew closer. A stream of dirt and gravel fell down in front of the boys. Someone was standing right on top of the ledge they were hiding under. Carlos hoped and prayed that no one could hear them panting.

"¿Dónde están?" a man's voice shouted. "Where are they?" Another voice answered in the distance and then another voice. Carlos could tell by the sounds that their pursuers had spread out. They heard the man above them walking away. Carlos felt like he could finally breathe easier.

"This is a great hiding hole," Miguel said in a tiny whisper.

"I know," Carlos replied. "We can hide here until they go away."

He shifted around in the hole so he would be more comfortable. He put his foot on a thick branch to brace himself. But suddenly the branch began to wobble and move. Carlos looked down to get a better footing when he realized the branch beneath his foot was sliding away. Just then the huge head of a brown snake whipped up into the air in front of both boys. The black beady eyes were staring straight at Carlos.

"Aaaaaaaaaaaaacccck!" Carlos screamed. Miguel's mouth was open but only made dry croaking noises. Two boys and a large snake all moved at the same time. Carlos jumped up out of the hole as if defying gravity. He tumbled over a boulder and down into the ravine. Miguel rolled right on top of him.

"¡Aquí, aquí!" a man's voice yelled above them. As Carlos scrambled to his feet, he saw the long shadow of a man. He looked up. It was the bearded man with the gun. Both boys ran back down the ravine.

Carlos had never run so fast in such a hard place to run. As the branches and limbs tore painfully at his clothes, he wondered if the snake had bitten him. He didn't think so, but everything had happened so quickly.

The ravine was a natural path compared to the jungle around them. The boys made better time than their pursuers. As the ravine leveled off, they came into a partially cleared field. Off to their right, Carlos saw some shacks.

"Santa Anita," Miguel said. "Run for it."

The boys sped across the field. Carlos glanced behind him but saw no one. He kept running. They came to a small garden behind the first house. They ran down between rows of corn. An old man was hoeing the garden.

"¿Tiene un teléfono?" Miguel asked.

"No tengo," the man said. "En la bodega."

"Maybe we should ask him to help us," Carlos said.

"I don't think we ought to risk it," Miguel replied. "Half these people probably work for Señora Garza already. I think we need to get to the phone first. We can call the police and the orphanage."

"You're probably right," Carlos agreed. They ran into the street.

"The bodega is down at the other end of town," Miguel said.

"We have to try to make it," Carlos said. "I don't want to go all the way back to Santiago on foot. I hope Rolando waited for us."

"Maybe they think we went the other way, down to the river," Miguel said. Carlos nodded. "I hope so."

The two boys walked rapidly up the street. Carlos looked down at his clothes. There were several tears and rips. Scratches covered his arms.

"You don't feel any snake bites, do you?" Carlos asked. He paused to look at his arms and legs. He had several scratches, some drawing blood.

"I don't think so," Miguel replied. Somehow that answer wasn't very comforting to Carlos.

"We better run," Carlos said after he had caught his breath. He began jogging. They passed several little houses. No one seemed to pay much attention to the strange boys. As they reached the top of the hill, they saw the bodega at the end of the village.

"There it is," Carlos said. But as soon as he finished speaking, a big black Cadillac turned on to the road. It drove down in front of the bodega and stopped. Señora Garza got out of the front seat of the car and went inside the bodega.

"Oh, no," Carlos said.

"We can still take the taxi," Miguel said. "Look. Rolando is still waiting."

"Yeah," Carlos replied. "But how will we get there without being seen? We can't just walk down the street. She'll see us."

"Oh, yes we can," Miguel said. He pointed behind them. A man and a boy were walking along with several burros down the middle of the street. When they passed the two boys, Miguel began following them. Carlos crouched down. The smelly burros were just tall enough to hide the two boys.

They ambled down the uneven street. Carlos was careful to avoid the mud holes. As they approached the end of the village, Señora Garza came out of the bodega. She looked all around and got back into her car. She closed the door, but the car didn't move. She was waiting.

Carlos felt more and more nervous as they got closer to the big black Cadillac. They were almost to Rolando's taxi. Both boys crouched down lower and lower. When the burros passed by the taxi, the two boys squatted down behind the trunk of the old car. They crawled around to the passenger side. Carlos opened the door slowly. Rolando woke from his napping with a start.

"Sssshhhh!" Miguel said to the old man. The two boys climbed into the back seat. Carlos eased the door shut.

"Take us back to town," Miguel whispered. The old man stared at the two boys' torn and dirty clothes. He sighed and reached down to start the car. The old engine moaned and groaned as it tried to start.

"Not again!" Carlos groaned as Rolando got out of the car. The old man walked slowly around and opened the hood. Carlos could hear metal clinking. Then Rolando got back into the car. The old man was humming as he tried the engine. After a few sputters and spurts, it roared to life.

"Finally," Carlos muttered.

"Look, there is Señora Garza's car," Rolando said. "She is waving at me."

"Please just go back to town," Carlos said. The old man turned the car around slowly in the street and headed back toward town. Both boys stayed down in the back seat. After a few moments, Carlos raised his head up slowly. They were almost at the end of the small village, rounding a curve. The road was wide open before him. He began to feel a wave of relief come over him when the Cadillac roared around the curve behind them. Señora Garza was at the wheel with a bearded man in a red shirt beside her. The Cadillac sped up.

"They're after us," Carlos yelled to Miguel. His friend popped his head up.

"Oh, no!" Miguel moaned. The black Cadillac surged forward, then suddenly it stopped.

"What's she doing?" Carlos asked.

"She's turning around," Miguel replied. "But why?"

"La policía," Rolando announced. Both boys turned around. The police car was coming rapidly up the road toward them with its red light flashing and siren blaring. Carlos turned back around. Señora Garza's black Cadillac roared back around the curve and out of sight.

"Stop the car!" Miguel yelled in Spanish. The old man did as he was told. Miguel opened the back door and hopped out. He waved his arms at the police car. Deputy Sánchez slowed down to a stop beside the old taxi. The siren slowly died to a low growl. Carlos hopped out of the other door.

Miguel was already talking to Deputy Sánchez. The deputy

looked amused and surprised.

"Tell him that they're taking drugs to the border," Carlos said.

"I did," Miguel replied.

"Tell them that they're hiding them in the piñatas," Carlos added

"I already did," Miguel responded.

"And tell him that Pastor Pablo and the other kids got the drugs by mistake."

"I'll tell him," Miguel said in frustration, "if you'll quit interrupting me."

Carlos waited patiently while Miguel poured out the whole story. The deputy nodded his head gravely. Carlos wished he understood Spanish better as the two talked.

"Deputy Sánchez wants us to go with him," Miguel said. The deputy went over to Rolando's taxi. He talked to the old man for a moment. Then the taxi slowly headed down the road. The two boys got into the police car. Deputy Sánchez got in. He turned off the blinking red light and drove toward Santa Anita.

"Where are we going?" Carlos asked.

"Back to the warehouse," Miguel replied.

"Do you think that's safe?" Carlos asked in alarm. "They had several men there. At least one has a gun."

"I told Deputy Sánchez that," Miguel replied. "He wants to get there before they can get rid of the drugs."

The police car roared back into the village. It sped down through the middle of the street.

"Shouldn't he use his radio and call for help?" Carlos asked. "Sheriff Vega should be here too."

"He doesn't seem too worried to me," Miguel replied.

The police car turned off the main street onto the little side road that led to the warehouse. A cold, scary feeling began to settle in Carlos's stomach as the tin building came into view. The black Cadillac was parked by the big truck. As the police car rolled to a stop, Deputy Sánchez pulled out his revolver. He looked in the back seat and smiled at the two boys. Then he got out of the car.

"Did you tell him that this was the street we were supposed to turn on to?" Carlos asked in a whisper. Miguel thought for a moment.

"I don't think so," he said.

"Then how did he know to come here?" Carlos asked.

"I'm not sure," Miguel replied.

Deputy Sánchez opened the boys' car door. Señora Garza came out of the building and walked over to Deputy Sánchez.

"Gracias," the big woman said to Deputy Sánchez.

"De nada," the deputy replied. He turned and smiled at the two boys. He motioned for them to get out of the car. Miguel and Carlos sat frozen in the back seat. Deputy Sánchez motioned again for them both to get out. This time his revolver pointed straight at them.

Chapter Ten

The Bragger Says Too Much

Qué buenos detectives," the deputy said with a smile as the boys slid out of the police car.

"Yeah, we're great detectives," Carlos said in disgust.

Two other men came out of the tin building with ropes. One walked over to Carlos and the other to Miguel. They pulled the boys' hands behind them. The rough rope burned Carlos's wrists as the man wrapped it around and pulled it tight.

"You won't get away with this," Carlos informed Señora Garza.

"Of course I will," the big woman said. "I've been doing it for some time already. Take them inside!"

The two men pushed Carlos and Miguel toward the tin

warehouse. Inside, all the workers were still busy transferring the drugs from the coffee sacks to the piñatas. Señora Garza led the boys to the far end of the building. The full piñatas were stacked all over the ground in a small mountain of bright colors and shapes. In front of them were boxes of fireworks. She made the boys sit on the dirt with their backs against the wall. A green lizard with a long tail scurried away. Deputy Sánchez followed them, still carrying his gun.

"What will you do with us?" Miguel asked fearfully.

"I haven't decided," the big woman said with a smile.

Roberto walked into the building. Señora Garza walked over to him. The two spoke together. Then they both walked back over to the two captives. Roberto smiled.

"So you caught these detectives!" the large boy said contemptuously. "I knew you would." He spat on Carlos and then spat on Miguel.

"My mother and father will figure out where I am," Carlos said bravely.

"I don't think so," the big woman said with a smile.

"You think you are so clever," Roberto said. "But I fooled you. I scared everybody. All those crybabies at the orphanage thought they were seeing ghosts. Now I will leave the orphanage and live with Señora Garza. She is going to adopt me."

"Is that why you betrayed all your friends?" Carlos asked. "Señora Garza will go to jail once they discover that she's responsible for Pastor Pablo and the children's overdosing on cocaine."

"That was a mistake," Señora Garza said hotly. "One of these stupid mountain women here wasn't careful. She put a piñata head that contained drugs on the body of a regular empty piñata. The pastor bought it at my store. Sorry for the mistake."

"They could have all died," Carlos spat out. "You're still in trouble, even if it was a mistake."

"It was a mistake," the big woman said with a smile. "But it was a good mistake. It only makes it easier to buy the orphanage. Half the people in town already believe Pastor Pablo did something wrong. Even if he doesn't go to jail, his reputation will be ruined. No one will ever know what really happened. They will be glad to see the 'haunted' orphanage shut down. Already some people in town are saying that the ghost gave him the drugs. I don't care. I will get everything I wanted, only much sooner than I planned."

"But why do you want to close the orphanage?" Carlos asked.

"Such a curious boy," Señora Garza said.

"He is just a nosy snoop," Roberto said. "But Señora Garza and I fooled you all."

"We tricked you into showing us where you hid your ghost costume," Carlos said defensively. "We saw you take it out of the pantry. And I know you made it look like Flaco stole those cassette tapes. You probably took the cassette recorder too."

"Everyone knows Flaco is a thief," Roberto said. The big boy laughed so hard his round cheeks shook.

"How did you know Roberto was the ghost?" Señora Garza asked with interest. "I must admit you are a clever boy."

"He is not as clever as me," Roberto insisted.

"The night we first saw the ghost, Flaco came up the road saying he was looking for Roberto," Carlos said to the big woman. "Later, Roberto came running down the road after us. It didn't seem right that none of us saw him until after we were all in the plaza. I began to suspect something then."

"Then what did you do?" Señora Garza asked.

"Later, when we saw the ghost at the window last night, I didn't remember seeing Flaco or Roberto. At that point I wondered if Flaco was somehow involved, but he seemed to be suspicious of Roberto too. Neither one seemed to like the other. I thought maybe he and Roberto were working together since they were roommates. Flaco was acting suspiciously."

"He knows nothing," Roberto scoffed. "He is so stupid. He'll go to jail for stealing. Deputy Sánchez will make sure of that."

"I wondered if Flaco was a thief too," Carlos said. "But we saw Flaco this morning at the same time that you said he stole the cassette tapes from your store. I figured if he didn't really steal the tapes, then Señora Garza must lying. I thought Roberto must be helping you since they found the items in Flaco's boxes. Somebody had to put them there. But I still wasn't sure."

Carlos stared at the big woman. She smiled uneasily. Deputy Sánchez looked at Carlos with new respect for the kid whose hands were tied.

"When we were in Roberto and Flaco's room, I found red mud inside the newspapers in the trash can," Carlos said. "I also found some wet shoes hidden under a box in his closet. There were bits of red mud left on them. The mud was the same kind that was outside the window where we saw the ghost. Since Flaco never wears shoes, I knew they belonged to Roberto. I figured that Roberto and Señora Garza were working together. But I wasn't sure why. So we tricked him. I thought he would get his costume and try to hide it somewhere else. When he ran into town, we followed him."

"You mean you came straight to town and didn't even stop to tell your mother or anyone?" Señora Garza asked as if she doubted Carlos.

"We had to come right away or we wouldn't see where Roberto went or what he did with the costume," Miguel added. The small boy cocked his head to one side to see better through the broken lens. "I helped Carlos figure all these things out too."

"You are also a clever boy," Señora Garza said, nodding her head up and down, staring back at the small boy.

"You think of everything," Roberto replied and laughed. "But you can't think yourselves free from those ropes."

Roberto walked over to the side of the room. He picked up a paper bag and opened it. He pulled out a long black sack and pulled it over his head. His arms stuck through holes in the side. He pulled the edge of the cloth across his chest. An off-white figure appeared on the boy's chest.

"Now you see the ghost," Roberto said, "and now you don't." He wrapped the black cloth over the figure.

"You were right about the ghost," Miguel said to Carlos. Roberto pulled the costume off and stuffed it back in the sack. He walked over to Carlos. He leaned closer and smiled.

"Boo!" Roberto yelled. Then the large boy kicked Carlos. "That's what you get for being so smart."

Pain ripped through Carlos's leg. Roberto danced around the two boys, gloating. Señora Garza watched the boy in silence.

"He is smart," Señora Garza said to Roberto. "He was able to follow us all the way here. You were a stupid boy to let him know so much! I'm not sure I want to adopt a foolish boy like you."

"It wasn't my fault." Roberto's happy face was suddenly gone.

"You were stupid to let him follow you," the woman said. "You were careless. We are lucky that he didn't talk to Sheriff Vega first."

"Don't yell at me." Roberto burst into tears. "I am not stupid! You said you would adopt me if I helped you. You promised!"

"¡Idiota!" Deputy Sánchez looked disgusted at Roberto. The boy wailed louder. Tears rolled down his full cheeks.

"Carlos is a smart boy," Señora Garza chided Roberto cruelly. "He figured out all your tricks in just two days."

"It's not my fault," Roberto wailed. "I did what you told me. I did everything."

Carlos almost felt sorry for Roberto, seeing his pitiful, tear-streaked face.

"You are a foolish boy," the big woman said slowly. "But at least you helped us find out what these boys know. They didn't tell anyone else. Now we can proceed without worry."

Carlos suddenly felt angry. Señora Garza smiled at him. He realized that the big woman had cleverly tricked him into telling her everything she wanted to know. He had wanted to prove to her and the others how clever he was, but he had said too much.

"I should have guessed that Deputy Sánchez was working with you," Carlos said softly.

"Yes, you should have," Señora Garza said. "You are not quite clever enough, are you? Come along, Roberto. Maybe you are more clever than these boys. Perhaps I will adopt you after all."

Roberto wiped his eyes and cheeks and ran over to the big woman. He tried to hug her, but she pushed him away. She barked out orders to the women filling the piñatas. Deputy

Sánchez and Roberto stayed by her side.

"I should have kept my big mouth shut," Carlos lamented. "I let her trick me."

"How could you keep quiet with Roberto teasing us like that?" Miguel demanded. "You had to tell."

"No, I didn't," Carlos moaned. "The Bible talks about the foolishness of boasting. Now she's not afraid. She'll do whatever she wants with us. No one knows we're here."

"What will she do?" Miguel asked fearfully.

"I don't know," Carlos said. "I don't want to think about it. We better pray hard."

"I've been praying."

"Me too." Carlos wriggled his hands. "These ropes are so tight, I think I'm losing the feeling in my fingers."

"We could try to run away," Miguel said wistfully.

"But the only door is down at their end. Even if we got past all of them, it would be hard to run with our hands behind our backs."

Down at the other end of the building, Señora Garza began to yell. Everyone stopped working. They gathered around a man with one of the large burlap sacks full of coffee beans. The big woman continued screaming.

"What's wrong?" Carlos asked.

"They're arguing about that sack of coffee beans," Miguel said. "Apparently it was opened before they got it off the truck. It was one of the last ones. Señora Garza wants to know if someone is stealing her drugs."

"Now they have to guess which thief and drug dealer is the most honest." Carlos twisted his hands. But the more he tried, the more the itchy rope burned into his wrists. The arguing at the other end of the building grew more intense. Everyone was trying to talk at once.

Carlos was watching the argument with great interest when he noticed the piñata on the floor beside him slowly move. He saw a long brown object moving underneath the brightly colored papier-mâché burro. He was about to scream that it was a snake when he saw fingers. Inside the fingers was a long knife.

"¡Silencio!" a voice whispered.

Carlos leaned around. The piñata rose up a little higher. He saw a face lying on the ground underneath it.

"Flaco!" Carlos whispered. The tall boy slid forward on his belly like a snake through a hole under the wall that Carlos and Miguel were leaning against.

"Sssshhhh," Flaco said. Miguel leaned forward to look around Carlos. Flaco spoke quickly and softly. Miguel just listened and nodded. Flaco slid back.

"He's going to cut the ropes," Miguel whispered. "Then he says we are to follow him. He's made a hole under the edge of the wall. If we crawl on our bellies, we can get out."

Carlos nodded. He felt the cold steel of the knife blade pressed between his hands. The ropes grew tighter for an instant. Then with a jerk his hands were free. He didn't move his arms. He waited until he could see that Miguel was also free.

"They'll still see us if we move too quickly" Carlos said. Miguel nodded and told Flaco what Carlos had said.

"He said we need to try, that it's our only chance," Miguel said.

"Wait a minute," Carlos said. "I've got an idea. Those crates over there are filled with fireworks. I've got matches in my right pocket. If Flaco can set them off, we might have a better chance of getting away."

Miguel whispered quickly to Flaco. The tall boy's eyes lit up when he heard the plan. He reached forward and put his hand into Carlos's pocket. He pulled out the book of matches.

Carlos quivered with fear. He didn't know if the plan would work or not. He turned his head. Flaco lit a match. But instead of tossing it into the nearest crate of fireworks, Flaco held it up to one of the piñatas. The brightly colored tissue caught fire quickly. Flaco lit another and another.

"Espérense," Flaco hissed.

" 'Wait,' " Miguel translated.

"Wait for what?" Carlos demanded in a frantic whisper. "Does he plan to go get hot dogs so we can roast them?"

The piñatas burned brighter. Flaco rose up slowly and pushed a whole stack of the papier-mâché figures on top of the ones already burning. Then he pushed the whole mound of figures toward the boxes of fireworks about ten feet away. One of the burning piñatas tumbled on top of the fireworks.

"¡Fuego!" a voice shouted at the other end of the room. "Fire!"

"Put it out!" Señora Garza screeched.

Other voices yelled out. The workers rushed forward. But the fireworks began to explode. Rockets whizzed and whistled as multicolored fountains of flames shot into the air. The whole room seemed to explode into a confusion of fire and screaming.

Chapter Eleven

Fire!

A wall of smoke and fire rose up before the boys. Behind the smoke, they could hear Señora Garza shouting orders. More boxes of fireworks began to explode. One rocket whizzed by Carlos's head.

"Let's get out of here!" Carlos cried out.

"¡Rápido!" Flaco yelled at the other boys above the shooting fireworks. The tall boy began crawling on his belly to show them the way out. Miguel crawled after him. Then came Carlos, following the soles of Miguel's shoes. By then the smoke was getting thick. Miguel squeezed through the hole under the wall. Carlos ducked down and was right behind him. He clawed at the sandy soil like a lizard. When his head popped out on the other side of the wall, he paused and took a deep breath of fresh air. But he didn't wait long. He grunted and pulled himself the rest of the way out. His pants were covered with black ash, but nothing was burning.

"Quickly!" Flaco said softly. He motioned for the boys to follow him into the dense brush and trees at the edge of the clearing. They started climbing the small hill. They were completely hidden by the time they were fifteen feet into the brush. They climbed higher and higher.

They finally stopped by some rocks. Sitting on the large boulders, they could look down at the tin building without being seen. But there was not much to worry about. Everyone was running around like crazy. Some were trying to fight the fire with a hose and buckets of water. Others were dragging crates of drugs and other items out of the warehouse. Loud bangs and whistles could be heard above the roar of the fire as more fireworks exploded.

"Maybe we should keep going," Miguel said as he caught his breath. "They may come after us."

"I don't think so," Carlos said with a smile. "The last time they saw us we were caught in the fire. I think we're safe. They won't discover we aren't in there until the fire is out. Flaco's plan was brilliant."

"You're right." Miguel smiled at their barefoot deliverer.

"But how did you know we were in there?" Carlos asked in amazement.

"I was sitting up here watching when they began chasing you the first time," Flaco said. "While most of them were out after you, I went down and spied on them from the same place you did earlier. I knew they had drugs in there, but I didn't know they were using the piñatas. I was still watching when Deputy Sánchez brought you back."

"The whole place might burn down," Miguel said in awe.

"I will thank God if it does," Flaco said and spat on the ground. "It's a house of death."

"How did you know they had drugs in there?" Carlos asked.

"Because my father used to work for Señora Garza," Flaco said bitterly. "Santa Anita is my home village. My father was a drunk and a bad man. That's why I came to live at the orphanage. My mother died of sickness, and my father was no father at all. All the people around here who work for Señora Garza are like slaves. But they are all afraid of her. Deputy Sánchez is in charge of this district, and Señora Garza bribes him."

"What about Chief Vega?" Carlos asked. "Is he corrupt too?"

"I hope not," Flaco replied. "At least Señor Gómez says he is not."

"What does Señor Gómez have to do with this?" Miguel asked.

"Señor Gómez knew that Señora Garza was doing evil things, but he couldn't prove it, and it was dangerous to try," Flaco said. "But today I gave him some proof. I went into the truck and opened one of the sacks of coffee beans. I found the drugs and took them to him."

"We saw you get into the truck," Carlos said with admiration. "But I had no idea what you were doing."

"I had been watching Señora Garza for several weeks, trying to figure out how she got the drugs," Flaco said bitterly. "Since I had lived in Santa Anita, I knew the drugs were coming from somewhere, I just didn't know how. Then today I heard about a strange boat at the docks. I went to look. No one notices a boy as much as they would a man. I hid on the boat and listened. Those men were half drunk, and they talked too much. They are from Colombia."

"Lots of drugs come out of Colombia," Carlos said. Flaco nodded.

"Señor Gómez knew the boat had coffee beans," Flaco said. "He went down there to try to buy some, but they refused to sell him any. He was very suspicious."

"So you got in the truck, opened a coffee bag and found the drugs," Carlos said.

"Yes, and I took them to Señor Gómez and told him where I found them," Flaco added. "Señor Gómez and I went together to Chief Vega and told him the whole story. Then I took a bus up to Santa Anita. I wanted to watch them to make sure they didn't get rid of the drugs too soon. Then you two came along."

"Then Chief Vega knows she is transporting drugs," Carlos said slowly. "But if he knows, why doesn't he do something?"

"He is," Flaco said. "He said he would need help. He said he would get the Federales, the government police, to help him."

"They are helping. Look!" Miguel exclaimed, pointing. All three boys looked down at the tin warehouse. Several police cars and over two dozen uniformed men holding rifles were rushing toward the burning building. They quickly surrounded it.

Not a shot was fired. Within a few moments, Señora Garza, Deputy Sánchez and all the others were brought into the clearing, holding up their hands. The Federal agents began handcuffing them. More police came down the tiny road in a long bus. Behind the bus, a van pulled into view.

"That's the van from the orphanage," Miguel said. Carlos's parents and Julie got out, followed by Señor Gómez and two old men.

"We better get down there," Carlos said.

The boys rushed down the hill through the thick brush. They raced across the clearing. They reached the crowd of police officers and their prisoners the same time as Carlos's parents arrived.

"Mom and Dad!"

"Carlos!" Pastor Brown yelled back. Carlos ran into his waiting arms. The whole family surrounded him with a hug.

"We thought you were in trouble," his mother said tearfully.

"We were for a while." Carlos replied.

"Rolando, the taxi driver, told Señor Gómez that Deputy Sánchez had taken you and Miguel," his mother said. "Señor Gómez told us about the drugs and the raid that Chief Vega was planning. We were worried sick."

"Your mother was about to make the Federales give her a rifle so she could go on the raid too," his dad said with a smile. He stared at their torn and dirty clothes with concern. "Are you sure you're all right?"

"We're okay," Carlos said. "Flaco saved us."

The tall boy smiled shyly as the others congratulated him. Señor Gómez patted Flaco on the head.

"He is a good boy," Señor Gómez said. "Very brave."

"Yes," a man said. Carlos turned around. A man with a blue patch over his eye came forward and patted Flaco on the back. Another man limped forward and did the same. Then he hugged Flaco.

"Who are those men?" Carlos whispered to his father.

"The man hugging Flaco is his father," his dad said. "The other man is his uncle."

"His father and uncle?" Carlos asked in surprise.

"Their names are Jorge and Marcos Hernández," his father replied.

"Make way! Make way!" Chief Vega said as he led the handcuffed prisoners across the clearing to be loaded onto the bus. Everyone stepped back. Señora Garza was the last in line. When she saw Carlos and Miguel, she cried out and gasped. The big woman stared at the boys in disbelief.

"What's the matter with her?" Julie asked.

"She probably thinks she's seeing ghosts," Carlos said. He, Flaco and Miguel began to laugh.

Chapter Twelve

The Power
to Change

The next day was Sunday. After the church service, all the children gathered in the big meeting hall. Many people from the town were there, including Señor Gómez and Chief Vega. The long tables were set with trays of food.

Pastor Pablo stood up to address the group. He looked pale, but he was steady on his feet. All the children had returned from the hospital except for Lucita, who was still recovering.

"We all owe a debt of gratitude to one of our own," Pastor Pablo said with a smile. "I'm sure you've all heard the story by now about how Flaco Hernández helped the police break up an evil group of drug dealers."

Pastor Pablo made Flaco stand up. The tall boy looked embarrassed as everyone cheered.

"But Flaco didn't act alone," Pastor Pablo said. "Carlos Brown and Miguel Romero also acted as very able detectives. In the last couple of days Carlos figured out how the children and I got sick from the drugs. As most of you have learned, they were stuffed into the head of the piñata from Isabel's birthday party. That head was supposed to be on the body of a parrot filled with drugs which would have been taken to the border. But apparently one of Señora Garza's workers made a mistake and put that head on a piñata that she sold in her store. I'm very thankful that God saved us from a terrible tragedy."

As Carlos and Miguel stood up, the crowd cheered once again. Carlos smiled. Miguel slapped his fellow detective on the back.

"Carlos also solved the problem of the so-called ghost that many of you saw," Pastor Pablo said with a smile.

Someone held up the ghost costume on a broom handle. The children booed and laughed. The police had recovered the ghost costume at the warehouse. All the children in the orphanage had seen it and how it worked the night before. Now no one believed in ghosts or that the orphanage or old church was haunted.

"There are other friends of the orphanage here today," Pastor Pablo said. "Señor Jorge Hernández and his brother, Marcos Hernández, also helped the police and the orphanage."

Pastor Pablo had the two men stand up. They had been sitting at the table next to Flaco and Señor Gómez.

"After Flaco came to live with us, I got to know these two men," Pastor Pablo said. "I told them how Jesus Christ died so they could be saved. They gave their lives to the Lord a few months ago, and their lives have been radically changed. They immediately quit working for Señora Garza. They also influenced others to quit working for her. Because of that, Señora Garza decided that we were dangerous. She was afraid that her ex-workers would begin to talk and expose her. She thought the best way to get rid of me was to shut down the orphanage. But these two men, filled with the Holy Spirit, kept testifying how Jesus had changed their lives. Now a whole community is being changed as others follow Jesus."

The whole room broke into applause and cheering. The two men smiled and sat down. Pastor Pablo prayed and the feasting began. Carlos and his family sat at the table with Flaco and his father and uncle.

Pastor Pablo came over and patted Flaco on the back. "We're going to miss having you at the orphanage."

"He's leaving?" Carlos asked with surprise.

"His father and uncle are going to work with Señor Gómez in his store," Pastor Pablo said. "Flaco is going back home to live with them."

"That's great," Carlos said.

"I will need more help with Señora Garza gone," Señor Gómez said with a smile. "She tried every evil trick to shut down my business. But now Chief Vega thinks I can buy her store and have two stores. I will be a very busy man."

"Señor Gómez will even help train some of the people in Santa Anita and help them sell their goods at the border," Chief Vega said. "Much of her business there was legitimate."

"What will happen to Señora Garza and the others?" Carlos asked.

"They will be in jail for a very long time," Chief Vega said.

"She was so greedy. That woman feared your power and influence in the lives of her workers so much that she became very desperate."

"It wasn't my power," Pastor Pablo said softly. "It was the power of the Holy Spirit she was fighting. He's the one who causes people to change."

"Yes." Carlos smiled. "And when you fight against God's power, you don't have a ghost of a chance."

**Don't miss the next book
in the Home School Detectives
series!**

**Here's a preview of
John Bibee's
*The Mystery of
the Campus Crook*.**

Chapter Two

Astrid

What do you want?" Emily looked nervously around the big room. Where was Josh? Where were the other people? Emily wished someone, anyone, would show up so she didn't have to be alone with this odd girl.

"I need your help," the girl replied.

"I don't know how I could help you," Emily said, dropping her music. "We are just here to play for the reception. My brother will back. The others will be here soon too."

"You'd have time to help me before the concert," the girl said eagerly. "I really would like your help. I can pay you some money."

"Pay me money?" Emily asked in surprise.

"For your services," the girl said. "You are one of those Home School Detectives, aren't you?"

"Well, yeah," Emily said slowly. "How did you know

about that?"

"Because I saw stories in the newspaper and your father has talked about you in class," the blond girl replied.

"You're one of my father's students?" Emily asked.

"Yes, and he's told us all about you and Josh and your friends and how you've helped solve crimes," the girl said. "He's bragged about all of you lots of times and put newspaper clippings on his bulletin board."

"I didn't know he talked about us in class too." Emily had finished picking up her music and now was sitting back in her chair.

"He's done it a number of times," the girl said seriously. "He's very proud of you. I wish my dad was that proud of me. I think everyone in my family is embarrassed that I exist."

"Oh," Emily said, unsure of what to say. The girl looked down at her feet, then looked back up.

"Will you help me?" she asked. "Like I said, I can pay, not a lot, but I could pay you a hundred dollars. And I'll pay you more if we're successful. I'm offering a reward."

"A hundred dollars?" Emily said. "We don't usually charge for helping people. It's not like we're professional detectives."

"But I would pay you," the girl insisted. "That's only fair. And I really could use your help."

Over the girl's shoulder, Emily saw Josh pulling a handcart carrying two black and gray amplifiers. Emily was never so glad to see Josh in her life.

"My brother's here," Emily said. "We need to set up for the reception."

"Yes, I know," the blond girl said. "That's why I came over here. Your father told me you would be here today."

"Did he say we would help you with detective work?" Emily asked.

"I didn't ask him about that," the blond girl replied. "He just said if we wanted to hear some good classical music to come to the reception. He's proud of your musical abilities too."

"Hi," Josh said as he wheeled the cart over to the little stage. He looked back and forth between Emily and the girl.

"My name is Astrid," the girl said, extending her hand. "Astrid Flacker."

"I'm Josh Morgan," Josh said. He shook her hand.

"Astrid wants to hire us as detectives," Emily said slowly. "She's in one of Daddy's classes. He's talked about us in class."

"The Home School Detectives are famous around campus," Astrid said. Then, for the first time, Emily saw Astrid smile. Even though she looked strange with her yellow-blond hair and earrings, she had a warm smile.

"How do you think we could we help you?" Josh asked curiously.

"I had a computer stolen," Astrid said seriously. "A notebook computer. I have to get it back. It has my master's thesis inside on the hard drive. It's life or death for me, at least for my academic career."

"You didn't make any backups?" Emily asked in surprise.

"I made three backups," Astrid said in anger. "I'm very careful to make backup copies. I'm an electrical engineering major. But all the copies were in my carrying case with the computer. I never thought it would get stolen. I have to get it back. The computer can be replaced, but not all my work. My notes and everything were on the computer."

"That's awful," Emily said sympathetically. "I lost a report I was doing one time. The power went off and I hadn't saved my work. But that was just a few hours of typing."

"This was work I've been doing for just over a year," Astrid said bitterly. "I was out with a friend having coffee. When I went back to my room, it was gone. It happened four days ago."

"Did you tell the police?"

"Yeah, sure," Astrid said with exasperation. "I told the campus police, and they filed a report with the city police. But they said not to get my hopes up. Something like a computer is hard to find. After I filed my report, they said there was nothing else they could do except notify me if it showed up."

"But you don't think that's going to happen?" Josh asked.

"It doesn't seem likely," Astrid replied. "But I've *got* to get my stuff back. At least I have to try."

"But how do you think we could help you?" Emily asked.

"Well, I've been asking questions around campus," Astrid said. "Since the campus police didn't seem to be making any progress, I decided to investigate myself."

"Sounds like you're a detective too," Josh said with a smile.

"Not by choice," Astrid said sadly. "It may be a waste of time, but I've got to get my computer back. I've offered rewards and put notices up on bulletin boards around campus and even on the electronic bulletin boards that I know the students use."

"A reward?" Emily asked.

"Yeah, I've offered a thousand dollars to someone if they'll give my computer back to me."

"Wow!" Josh said. "That's a lot of money."

"The work on my thesis is worth a lot more than that to me," Astrid said anxiously.

"But how can we help you if the police can't?" Emily asked.

"That's the tricky part," Astrid said. "Like I told you, I've been snooping around. I think I might know who stole my computer."

"Then why don't you just tell the police?" Josh asked. "Couldn't they get it back?"

"Well, I'm not exactly sure who has it," Astrid said with a frown. "You have to be pretty sure for the police to do much."

"How could we help you?" Josh asked.

"I want to investigate some on my own, but I sort of need some friends or partners to help me investigate," Astrid replied.

"Why wouldn't you just use some of your friends on campus to help you?" Josh asked.

"Because I'm not sure who my real friends are anymore," Astrid said bitterly. "In fact, I think it might have been some of my friends who stole my computer. I don't know who I can trust anymore. That's when I thought of you guys. I know you can be trusted."

"You mean your own friends would steal from you?" Emily asked.

"Maybe," Astrid said.

"Sounds like you could use some new friends," Josh added.

"Yeah, I know that now," Astrid said, her voice cracking with anger. "Won't you please help me? Like I said, I'll pay you just to help. And besides, I'll even give you the reward if we find the computer. A thousand dollars."

"I'd like to help you," Emily said. "And you don't need to pay us anything, does she, Josh?"

"We don't usually work for money," Josh said. "But we do have our concert performance at the reception. That's why we're here."

"We could do it before the concert," Astrid said eagerly. "If we're lucky, I'll just need you for about twenty minutes, tops."

"You mean you don't want us to look for clues?" Emily asked.

"Not at all," Astrid said. "I just need you to help me look for clues."

"How can we do that?" Josh asked.

"I have a plan, but I need someone to help me with it," Astrid said. "There's a place just a few blocks from here where I want to look for my computer. Please help me. I really need someone and I don't know who else to turn to."

"We have time, don't we, Josh?" Emily said. She felt sorry for the girl, especially since it was a computer that had been stolen.

"I guess so," Josh said with a frown. "I'm still not sure what you want us to do if we're not looking for clues."

"Just come with me, and I'll explain it when we get there," Astrid said. "Please."

"I'd like to help you," Emily said eagerly. "I would hate it if someone stole my computer. What kind of laptop did you have?"

"A Toshiba," Astrid said. "I've had three of them over the years, and they're great. I kept upgrading to new models every few years."

"Did it have a color or mono monitor?"

"Color, with a gigabyte hard drive, thirty-two megs of memory," Astrid said. "And a twenty-eight-point-eight modem."

"Wow, that sounds like a powerful setup."

"It was a *great* computer," Astrid said sadly. She looked back and forth between Emily and Josh impatiently. "Will you help? Please?"

"Let's go then," Josh said. "But we can't stay too long."

"Great," Astrid said. Josh pushed the handcart behind the little stage and left it. As they walked toward the elevators, two men entered the room talking furiously. One was an older man with short gray hair and an expensive suit. The other was much younger, very tall and big. The younger man wore a gray uniform-type jacket. A badge on the jacket said *Rod Williams: Museum Guard.*

"I'm going to pull my hair out if that stupid fire alarm goes off one more time," the older man said. "Yesterday was the third false alarm, and the fire department is tired of coming down here every fifteen minutes."

"I don't like it either," the big guard said. "But hey, I'm just a guard. I don't understand those electronic things."

"I know," the older man said with a sigh. When he saw Josh and Emily, his face lit up with a smile.

"Josh and Emily Morgan," the older man said. "It's so good to see you again."

"Hi, Mr. Bunson," Josh said. Mr. Bunson was the assistant director of the museum. He looked very small next to the big guard.

"We're looking forward to great music today," Mr. Bunson said. "I was telling Rod earlier about your musical abilities."

"Thanks," Emily said. The big guard smiled easily. He stared at Astrid for a moment, looking especially at her wild blond hair.

"Did you say the fire alarm went off?" Josh asked.

"Yes," Mr. Bunson said. "It's been a nightmare. All false alarms. We don't know if it's been from the thunderstorms or power surges or what's causing them. But they've been an absolute nuisance. Three false alarms in two days."

Three women walked into the room. They each wore a pretty pastel dress and lots of heavy, sparkling jewelry.

"Hello, Mrs. Bunson," Emily said to the woman in blue.

"Hello, dear," Mrs. Bunson said sweetly. "You make our little fundraising events that much more special. I've told everyone to expect a top-notch performance at the reception."

"We'll do our best," Josh said. The other women looked at Astrid with blank stares. One frowned, looking at all the earrings in her ear.

"We need to run," Emily said.

"All right, children," Mrs. Bunson said. "We'll see you in a little while."

Astrid led the way. They went upstairs in the elevators. As they walked out into the big exhibition hall, the room seemed more full than ever. More students had arrived. The big room echoed with noisy voices.

"Can you wait here?" Astrid asked seriously. "I need to use the restroom."

"We'll wait," Emily said.

"Thanks," Astrid said. She walked quickly away.

Several university students with bright blue jackets were acting as tour guides for the exhibit. Emily recognized one of the student tour guides, Wendy Phillips, as a member of their church in Springdale. She was a beautiful girl with long red hair and a wonderful smile. She was also a school cheerleader.

She waved at Emily. Emily smiled and waved back. She was glad that Wendy had noticed her.

"That's Wade Wyoming next to Wendy," Josh said.

"Who's he?"

"Who's he?" Josh repeated in surprise. "He's the star quarterback of the football team. He'll probably get drafted on a pro team. He's been out of action the last few weeks because his arm is hurt. But he should be back soon."

"He sure is big," Emily said, looking at the tall, handsome student.

"Hey, Wade!" Josh yelled across the room. Wade flashed a smile at Josh and waved back.

"Does he know you?" Emily asked.

"Of course not," Josh said. "But it looks like he knows Wendy."

"Yeah," Emily said, noticing that Wade and Wendy were leading a tour group together. Lots of young schoolchildren also knew about Wade. Some were asking him for autographs. Josh was tempted to go get an autograph himself, especially when it was almost a sure thing that the quarterback would be drafted into the NFL someday.

"Do you think we can really help Astrid get her computer back?" Emily asked.

"I don't know," Josh said with a frown. "She seems odd to me."

"I think she really needs our help," Emily said. "You can't tell everything about someone just by their appearance. She is one of Daddy's students."

"I know," Josh said. "I just have a feeling there's more to this story than we're getting. I still don't understand what we're supposed to do."

"Here she comes," Emily said. "I guess we'll find out about her plan soon enough."

"I'm ready," Astrid said seriously. "Let's go."

The blond student led the way out through the big hall toward the front doors. They had to wait at the door as another whole busload of students filed inside. After they passed, Astrid motioned for them to go outside.

Outside, the sky was getting darker and cloudier. Astrid frowned at the clouds. "I hope it doesn't rain on us," she said. "But it's only a few blocks from here, anyway. Follow me."

Astrid crossed the green lawn around the art museum. She walked faster than most people, and Emily almost had to run to keep up. They passed the big natural history and science museum. The young woman led the way across the parking lot to the street. They walked down the sidewalk for a block and then crossed the street.

"It's right over there on the next block," Astrid said.

"What?"

"That big house," Astrid said. "We're off campus now, but that's a fraternity house."

"What's a fraternity?" Emily asked.

"It's a kind of student social club," Josh said. "They usually have Greek alphabet letters as the names of the clubs. Men are in fraternities and women are in sororities, right?"

"Yes," Astrid said. "Most members of fraternities live in the big fraternity houses instead of the dorms or apartments."

"Are you in a sorority?" Emily asked.

"They don't let people like me in clubs like that," Astrid said seriously. "In fact, that's why I need you two to help me."

"I still don't understand what you want us to do," Josh said as they walked across the street toward the fraternity house.

"Let's go around to the side," Astrid said mysteriously as they got near the big three-story house. Three tall oak trees stood proudly in the front lawn.

"That's a huge house," Emily said as they followed Astrid. The third story had a balcony. A huge trellis with rosebushes climbed up the side of the house.

"What do you want us to do?" Josh asked.

"Inside the front door there's a desk, and there will be a guy behind the desk," Astrid said. "I want you to go inside and give him this envelope. The guy's name is Carl."

The blond girl pulled a plain white envelope out of her back pocket. She gave it to Emily. *Carl* was written on the outside of the envelope.

"What's in it?" Josh asked.

"Just a note," Astrid said. She looked at her watch. "Please help me. But don't tell him I gave you the note."

"Just give him this envelope, and ask him to read it?" Josh asked. "And you don't want us to tell him you gave it to us."

"That's all I need," Astrid said, her eyes pleading.

"This is kind of strange detective work," Josh said slowly. "I guess that's the way it happens sometimes."

"I'll give him the note," Emily said.

"Don't tell him it's from me or even mention me, please," Astrid added. "It won't work if they think I'm around."

"Okay," Emily said. Astrid stood behind a big oak tree near a corner of the house.

"This seems pretty weird," Josh muttered as they walked up the steps of the big house.

"I think it's kind of mysterious and exciting," Emily said. "It's like being detectives on television."

"I don't know," Josh said warily.

They opened the big front door on the house and walked inside. Just like Astrid had told them, a student was sitting behind a desk in front of a big set of wooden stairs. A large living room with three couches and some chairs and a big television were off to the right. A hallway led down to the left.

"Are you Carl?" Emily asked.

"Yes," he said with a handsome smile.

"We have this note for you," Emily said, handing the note across the countertop.

"A note?" Carl asked. He took the envelope. He opened it and read it.

"He must be real busy today," Carl said. "Thank you, tell him I'll check it out. He must have been too busy to call if he sent you two with a note."

He looked with a questioning face at Emily.

"I guess," Emily said, shrugging her shoulders.

"I'll take care of it," Carl said with a smile. He stood up and started down the hallway. Emily and Josh stood in front of the desk. Carl looked at them with surprise. "You can tell him I'll check it out, okay? Bye."

Carl turned and walked down the hall. The lobby was empty. "I guess we just go now," Josh said.

"Okay," Emily added. They turned to open the front door. As they walked out, Astrid darted up the steps.

"I'll meet you back at the museum later," Astrid whispered as she rushed past them. She walked quickly around the desk and then started up the stairs. She only stopped for a second to look back at the surprised faces of Emily and Josh. She held her finger up to her lips, as if telling them to be quiet, then waved her hand as if to shoo them away. Then she turned and tiptoed up the broad wooden stairs until she was out of sight.